The Line of Love

The Line of Love

James Branch Cabell

MINT EDITIONS

The Line of Love was first published in 1905.

This edition published by Mint Editions 2021.

ISBN 9781513295725 | E-ISBN 9781513297224

Published by Mint Editions®

 MINT
EDITIONS
minteditionbooks.com

Publishing Director: Jennifer Newens
Design & Production: Rachel Lopez Metzger
Project Manager: Micaela Clark
Typesetting: Westchester Publishing Services

Contents

The Epistle Dedicatory

"In elect utteraunce to make memoriall,
To thee for souccour, to thee for helpe I call,
Mine homely rudeness and dryghness to expell
With the freshe waters of Elyconys well."

MY DEAR MRS. GRUNDY

You may have observed that nowadays we rank the love-story among the comfits of literature; and we do this for the excellent reason that man is a thinking animal by courtesy rather than usage.

Rightly considered, the most trivial love-affair is of staggering import. Who are we to question this, when nine-tenths of us owe our existence to a summer flirtation? And while our graver economic and social and psychic "problems" (to settle some one of which is nowadays the object of all ponderable fiction) are doubtless worthy of most serious consideration, you will find, my dear madam, that frivolous love-affairs, little and big, were shaping history and playing spillikins with sceptres long before any of these delectable matters were thought of.

Yes, even the most talked-about "questions of the day" are sometimes worthy of consideration; but were it not for the kisses of remote years and the high gropings of hearts no longer animate, there would be none to accord them this same consideration, and a void world would teeter about the sun, silent and naked as an orange. Love is an illusion, if you will; but always through this illusion, alone, has the next generation been rendered possible, and all endearing human idiocies, including "questions of the day," have been maintained.

Love, then, is no trifle. And literature, mimicking life at a respectful distance, may very reasonably be permitted an occasional reference to the corner-stone of all that exists. For in life "a trivial little love-story" is a matter more frequently aspersed than found. Viewed in the light of its consequences, any love-affair is of gigantic signification, inasmuch as the most trivial is a part of Nature's unending and, some say, her only labor, toward the peopling of the worlds.

She is uninventive, if you will, this Nature, but she is tireless. Generation by generation she brings it about that for a period weak men may stalk as demigods, while to every woman is granted at least one hour wherein to spurn the earth, a warm, breathing angel. Generation by generation does Nature thus betrick humanity, that humanity may endure.

Here for a little—with the gracious connivance of Mr. R. E. Townsend, to whom all lyrics hereinafter should be accredited—I have followed Nature, the arch-trickster. Through her monstrous tapestry I have traced out for you the windings of a single thread. It is particolored, this thread—now black for a mourning sign, and now scarlet where blood has stained it, and now brilliancy itself—for the tinsel of young love (if, as wise men tell us, it be but tinsel), at least makes a prodigiously fine appearance until time tarnish it. I entreat you, dear lady, to accept this traced-out thread with assurances of my most distinguished regard.

The gift is not great. Hereinafter is recorded nothing more weighty than the follies of young persons, perpetrated in a lost world which when compared with your ladyship's present planet seems rather callow. Hereinafter are only love-stories, and nowadays nobody takes love-making very seriously. . .

And truly, my dear madam, I dare say the Pompeiians did not take Vesuvius very seriously; it was merely an eligible spot for a *fête champêtre*. And when gaunt fishermen first preached Christ about the highways, depend upon it, that was not taken very seriously, either. *Credat Judaeus*; but all sensible folk—such as you and I, my dear madam—passed on with a tolerant shrug, knowing "their doctrine could be held of no sane man."

APRIL 30, 1293 — MAY 1, 1323

"Pus vezem de novelh florir pratz, e vergiers reverdezir rius e fontanas esclarzir, ben deu quascus lo joy jauzir don es jauzens."

It would in ordinary circumstances be my endeavor to tell you, first of all, just whom the following tale concerns. Yet to do this is not expedient, since any such attempt could not but revive the question as to whose son was Florian de Puysange?

No gain is to be had by resuscitating the mouldy scandal: and, indeed, it does not matter a button, nowadays, that in Poictesme, toward the end of the thirteenth century, there were elderly persons who considered the young Vicomte de Puysange to exhibit an indiscreet resemblance to Jurgen the pawnbroker. In the wild youth of Jurgen, when Jurgen was a practising poet (declared these persons), Jurgen had been very intimate with the former Vicomte de Puysange, now dead, for the two men had much in common. Oh, a great deal more in common, said these gossips, than the poor vicomte ever suspected, as you can see for yourself. That was the extent of the scandal, now happily forgotten, which we must at outset agree to ignore.

All this was in Poictesme, whither the young vicomte had come a-wooing the oldest daughter of the Comte de la Forêt. The whispering and the nods did not much trouble Messire Jurgen, who merely observed that he was used to the buffets of a censorious world; young Florian never heard of this furtive chatter; and certainly what people said in Poictesme did not at all perturb the vicomte's mother, that elderly and pious lady, Madame Félise de Puysange, at her remote home in Normandy. The principals taking the affair thus quietly, we may with profit emulate them. So I let lapse this delicate matter of young Florian's paternity, and begin with his wedding.

I

The Episode Called The Wedding Jest

1. *Concerning Several Compacts*

It is a tale which they narrate in Poictesme, telling how love began between Florian de Puysange and Adelaide de la Forêt. They tell also how young Florian had earlier fancied other women for one reason or another; but that this, he knew, was the great love of his life, and a love which would endure unchanged as long as his life lasted.

And the tale tells how the Comte de la Forêt stroked a gray beard, and said, "Well, after all, Puysange is a good fief—"

"As if that mattered!" cried his daughter, indignantly. "My father, you are a deplorably sordid person."

"My dear," replied the old gentleman, "it does matter. Fiefs last."

So he gave his consent to the match, and the two young people were married on Walburga's Eve, on the day that ends April.

And they narrate how Florian de Puysange was vexed by a thought that was in his mind. He did not know what this thought was. But something he had overlooked; something there was he had meant to do, and had not done: and a troubling consciousness of this lurked at the back of his mind like a small formless cloud. All day, while bustling about other matters, he had groped toward this unapprehended thought.

Now he had it: Tiburce.

The young Vicomte de Puysange stood in the doorway, looking back into the bright hall where they of Storisende were dancing at his marriage feast. His wife, for a whole half-hour his wife, was dancing with handsome Etienne de Nérac. Her glance met Florian's, and Adelaide flashed him an especial smile. Her hand went out as though to touch him, for all that the width of the hall severed them.

Florian remembered presently to smile back at her. Then he went out of the castle into a starless night that was as quiet as an unvoiced menace. A small and hard and gnarled-looking moon ruled over the dusk's secrecy. The moon this night, afloat in a luminous gray void, somehow reminded Florian of a glistening and unripe huge apple.

The foliage about him moved at most as a sleeper breathes, while Florian descended eastward through walled gardens, and so came to the graveyard. White mists were rising, such mists as the witches of Amneran notoriously evoked in these parts on each Walburga's Eve to purchase recreations which squeamishness leaves undescribed.

For five years now Tiburce d'Arnaye had lain there. Florian thought of his dead comrade and of the love which had been between them—a love more perfect and deeper and higher than commonly exists between men—and the thought came to Florian, and was petulantly thrust away, that Adelaide loved ignorantly where Tiburce d'Arnaye had loved with comprehension. Yes, he had known almost the worst of Florian de Puysange, this dear lad who, none the less, had flung himself between Black Torrismond's sword and the breast of Florian de Puysange. And it seemed to Florian unfair that all should prosper with him, and Tiburce lie there imprisoned in dirt which shut away the color and variousness of things and the drollness of things, wherein Tiburce d'Arnaye had taken such joy. And Tiburce, it seemed to Florian—for this was a strange night—was struggling futilely under all that dirt, which shut out movement, and clogged the mouth of Tiburce, and would not let him speak; and was struggling to voice a desire which was unsatisfied and hopeless.

"O comrade dear," said Florian, "you who loved merriment, there is a feast afoot on this strange night, and my heart is sad that you are not here to share in the feasting. Come, come, Tiburce, a right trusty friend you were to me; and, living or dead, you should not fail to make merry at my wedding."

Thus he spoke. White mists were rising, and it was Walburga's Eve.

So a queer thing happened, and it was that the earth upon the grave began to heave and to break in fissures, as when a mole passes through the ground. And other queer things happened after that, and presently Tiburce d'Arnaye was standing there, gray and vague in the moonlight as he stood there brushing the mold from his brows, and as he stood there blinking bright wild eyes. And he was not greatly changed, it seemed to Florian; only the brows and nose of Tiburce cast no shadows upon his face, nor did his moving hand cast any shadow there, either, though the moon was naked overhead.

"You had forgotten the promise that was between us," said Tiburce; and his voice had not changed much, though it was smaller.

"It is true. I had forgotten. I remember now." And Florian shivered a little, not with fear, but with distaste.

"A man prefers to forget these things when he marries. It is natural enough. But are you not afraid of me who come from yonder?"

"Why should I be afraid of you, Tiburce, who gave your life for mine?"

"I do not say. But we change yonder."

"And does love change, Tiburce? For surely love is immortal."

"Living or dead, love changes. I do not say love dies in us who may hope to gain nothing more from love. Still, lying alone in the dark clay, there is nothing to do, as yet, save to think of what life was, and of what sunlight was, and of what we sang and whispered in dark places when we had lips; and of how young grass and murmuring waters and the high stars beget fine follies even now; and to think of how merry our loved ones still contrive to be, even now, with their new playfellows. Such reflections are not always conducive to philanthropy."

"Tell me," said Florian then, "and is there no way in which we who are still alive may aid you to be happier yonder?"

"Oh, but assuredly," replied Tiburce d'Arnaye, and he discoursed of curious matters; and as he talked, the mists about the graveyard thickened. "And so," Tiburce said, in concluding his tale, "it is not permitted that I make merry at your wedding after the fashion of those who are still in the warm flesh. But now that you recall our ancient compact, it is permitted I have my peculiar share in the merriment, and I may drink with you to the bride's welfare."

"I drink," said Florian, as he took the proffered cup, "to the welfare of my beloved Adelaide, whom alone of women I have really loved, and whom I shall love always."

"I perceive," replied the other, "that you must still be having your joke."

Then Florian drank, and after him Tiburce. And Florian said, "But it is a strange drink, Tiburce, and now that you have tasted it you are changed."

"You have not changed, at least," Tiburce answered; and for the first time he smiled, a little perturbingly by reason of the change in him.

"Tell me," said Florian, "of how you fare yonder."

So Tiburce told him of yet more curious matters. Now the augmenting mists had shut off all the rest of the world. Florian could see only vague rolling graynesses and a gray and changed Tiburce sitting there, with bright wild eyes, and discoursing in a small chill voice. The appearance of a woman came, and sat beside him on the right. She, too, was gray, as became Eve's senior: and she made a sign which Florian remembered, and it troubled him.

Tiburce said then, "And now, young Florian, you who were once so dear to me, it is to your welfare I drink."

"I drink to yours, Tiburce."

Tiburce drank first: and Florian, having drunk in turn, cried out, "You have changed beyond recognition!"

"You have not changed," Tiburce d'Arnaye replied again. "Now let me tell you of our pastimes yonder."

With that he talked of exceedingly curious matters. And Florian began to grow dissatisfied, for Tiburce was no longer recognizable, and Tiburce whispered things uncomfortable to believe; and other eyes, as wild as his, but lit with red flarings from behind, like a beast's eyes, showed in the mists to this side and to that side, for unhappy beings were passing through the mists upon secret errands which they discharged unwillingly. Then, too, the appearance of a gray man now sat to the left of that which had been Tiburce d'Arnaye, and this newcomer was marked so that all might know who he was: and Florian's heart was troubled to note how handsome and how admirable was that desecrated face even now.

"But I must go," said Florian, "lest they miss me at Storisende, and Adelaide be worried."

"Surely it will not take long to toss off a third cup. Nay, comrade, who were once so dear, let us two now drink our last toast together. Then go, in Sclaug's name, and celebrate your marriage. But before that let us drink to the continuance of human mirth-making everywhere."

Florian drank first. Then Tiburce took his turn, looking at Florian as Tiburce drank slowly. As he drank, Tiburce d'Arnaye was changed even more, and the shape of him altered, and the shape of him trickled as though Tiburce were builded of sliding fine white sand. So Tiburce d'Arnaye returned to his own place. The appearances that had sat to his left and to his right were no longer there to trouble Florian with memories. And Florian saw that the mists of Walburga's Eve had departed, and that the sun was rising, and that the graveyard was all overgrown with nettles and tall grass.

He had not remembered the place being thus, and it seemed to him the night had passed with unnatural quickness. But he thought more of the fact that he had been beguiled into spending his wedding-night in a graveyard, in such questionable company, and of what explanation he could make to Adelaide.

2. Of Young Persons in May

THE TALE TELLS HOW FLORIAN DE PUYSANGE came in the dawn through flowering gardens, and heard young people from afar, already about their maying. Two by two he saw them from afar as they went with romping and laughter into the tall woods behind Storisende to fetch back the May-pole with dubious old rites. And as they went they sang, as was customary, that song which Raimbaut de Vaqueiras made in the ancient time in honor of May's ageless triumph.

Sang they:

> *"May shows with godlike showing*
> *Today for each that sees*
> *May's magic overthrowing*
> *All musty memories*
> *In him whom May decrees*
> *To be love's own. He saith,*
> *'I wear love's liveries*
> *Until released by death.'"*

> *"Thus all we laud May's sowing,*
> *Nor heed how harvests please*
> *When nowhere grain worth growing*
> *Greets autumn's questing breeze,*
> *And garnerers garner these—*
> *Vain words and wasted breath*
> *And spilth and tasteless lees—*
> *Until released by death."*

> *"Unwillingly foreknowing*
> *That love with May-time flees,*
> *We take this day's bestowing,*
> *And feed on fantasies*
> *Such as love lends for ease*
> *Where none but travaileth,*

With lean infrequent fees,
Until released by death."

And Florian shook his sleek black head. "A very foolish and pessimistical old song, a superfluous song, and a song that is particularly out of place in the loveliest spot in the loveliest of all possible worlds."

Yet Florian took no inventory of the gardens. There was but a happy sense of green and gold, with blue topping all; of twinkling, fluent, tossing leaves and of the gray under side of elongated, straining leaves; a sense of pert bird noises, and of a longer shadow than usual slanting before him, and a sense of youth and well-being everywhere. Certainly it was not a morning wherein pessimism might hope to flourish.

Instead, it was of Adelaide that Florian thought: of the tall, impulsive, and yet timid, fair girl who was both shrewd and innocent, and of her tenderly colored loveliness, and of his abysmally unmerited felicity in having won her. Why, but what, he reflected, grimacing—what if he had too hastily married somebody else? For he had earlier fancied other women for one reason or another: but this, he knew, was the great love of his life, and a love which would endure unchanged as long as his life lasted.

3. *What Comes of Marrying Happily*

THE TALE TELLS HOW FLORIAN DE PUYSANGE found Adelaide in the company of two ladies who were unknown to him. One of these was very old, the other an imposing matron in middle life. The three were pleasantly shaded by young oak-trees; beyond was a tall hedge of clipped yew. The older women were at chess, while Adelaide bent her meek golden head to some of that fine needlework in which the girl delighted. And beside them rippled a small sunlit stream, which babbled and gurgled with silver flashes. Florian hastily noted these things as he ran laughing to his wife.

"Heart's dearest—!" he cried. And he saw, perplexed, that Adelaide had risen with a faint wordless cry, and was gazing at him as though she were puzzled and alarmed a very little.

"Such an adventure as I have to tell you of!" says Florian then.

"But, hey, young man, who are you that would seem to know my daughter so well?" demands the lady in middle life, and she rose majestically from her chess-game.

Florian stared, as he well might. "Your daughter, madame! But certainly you are not Dame Melicent."

At this the old, old woman raised her nodding head. "Dame Melicent? And was it I you were seeking, sir?"

Now Florian looked from one to the other of these incomprehensible strangers, bewildered: and his eyes came back to his lovely wife, and his lips smiled irresolutely. "Is this some jest to punish me, my dear?"

But then a new and graver trouble kindled in his face, and his eyes narrowed, for there was something odd about his wife also.

"I have been drinking in queer company," he said. "It must be that my head is not yet clear. Now certainly it seems to me that you are Adelaide de la Forêt, and certainly it seems to me that you are not Adelaide."

The girl replied, "Why, no, messire; I am Sylvie de Nointel."

"Come, come," says the middle-aged lady, briskly, "let us make an end to this play-acting, and, young fellow, let us have a sniff at you. No, you are not tipsy, after all. Well, I am glad of that. So let us get to the bottom of this business. What do they call you when you are at home?"

"Florian de Puysange," he answered, speaking meekly enough. This capable large person was to the young man rather intimidating.

"La!" said she. She looked at him very hard. She nodded gravely two or three times, so that her double chin opened and shut. "Yes, and you favor him. How old are you?"

He told her twenty-four.

She said, inconsequently: "So I was a fool, after all. Well, young man, you will never be as good-looking as your father, but I trust you have an honester nature. However, bygones are bygones. Is the old rascal still living? and was it he that had the impudence to send you to me?"

"My father, madame, was slain at the battle of Marchfeld—"

"Some fifty years ago! And you are twenty-four. Young man, your parentage had unusual features, or else we are at cross-purposes. Let us start at the beginning of this. You tell us you are called Florian de Puysange and that you have been drinking in queer company. Now let us have the whole story."

Florian told of last night's happenings, with no more omissions than seemed desirable with feminine auditors.

Then the old woman said: "I think this is a true tale, my daughter, for the witches of Amneran contrive strange things, with mists to aid them, and with Lilith and Sclaug to abet. Yes, and this fate has fallen before to men that were over-friendly with the dead."

"Stuff and nonsense!" said the stout lady.

"But, no, my daughter. Thus seven persons slept at Ephesus, from the time of Decius to the time of Theodosius—"

"Still, Mother—"

"—And the proof of it is that they were called Constantine and Dionysius and John and Malchus and Marcian and Maximian and Serapion. They were duly canonized. You cannot deny that this thing happened without asserting no less than seven blessed saints to have been unprincipled liars, and that would be a very horrible heresy—"

"Yet, Mother, you know as well as I do—"

"—And thus Epimenides, another excellently spoken-of saint, slept at Athens for fifty-seven years. Thus Charlemagne slept in the Untersberg, and will sleep until the ravens of Miramon Lluagor have left his mountains. Thus Rhyming Thomas in the Eildon Hills, thus Ogier in Avalon, thus Oisin—"

The old lady bade fair to go on interminably in her gentle resolute piping old voice, but the other interrupted.

"Well, Mother, do not excite yourself about it, for it only makes your asthma worse, and does no especial good to anybody. Things may be as you say. Certainly I intended nothing irreligious. Yet these extended naps, appropriate enough for saints and emperors, are out of place in one's own family. So, if it is not stuff and nonsense, it ought to be. And that I stick to."

"But we forget the boy, my dear," said the old lady. "Now listen, Florian de Puysange. Thirty years ago last night, to the month and the day, it was that you vanished from our knowledge, leaving my daughter a forsaken bride. For I am what the years have made of Dame Melicent, and this is my daughter Adelaide, and yonder is her daughter Sylvie de Nointel."

"La, Mother," observed the stout lady, "but are you certain it was the last of April? I had been thinking it was some time in June. And I protest it could not have been all of thirty years. Let me see now, Sylvie, how old is your brother Richard? Twenty-eight, you say. Well, Mother, I always said you had a marvelous memory for things like that, and I often envy you. But how time does fly, to be sure!"

And Florian was perturbed. "For this is an awkward thing, and Tiburce has played me an unworthy trick. He never did know when to leave off joking; but such posthumous frivolity is past endurance. For, see now, in what a pickle it has landed me! I have outlived my friends,

I may encounter difficulty in regaining my fiefs, and certainly I have lost the fairest wife man ever had. Oh, can it be, madame, that you are indeed my Adelaide!"

"Yes, every pound of me, poor boy, and that says much."

"—And that you have been untrue to the eternal fidelity which you vowed to me here by this very stream! Oh, but I cannot believe it was thirty years ago, for not a grass-blade or a pebble has been altered; and I perfectly remember the lapping of water under those lichened rocks, and that continuous file of ripples yonder, which are shaped like arrowheads."

Adelaide rubbed her nose. "Did I promise eternal fidelity? I can hardly remember that far back. But I remember I wept a great deal, and my parents assured me you were either dead or a rascal, so that tears could not help either way. Then Ralph de Nointel came along, good man, and made me a fair husband, as husbands go—"

"As for that stream," then said Dame Melicent, "it is often I have thought of that stream, sitting here with my grandchildren where I once sat with gay young men whom nobody remembers now save me. Yes, it is strange to think that instantly, and within the speaking of any simple word, no drop of water retains the place it had before the word was spoken: and yet the stream remains unchanged, and stays as it was when I sat here with those young men who are gone. Yes, that is a strange thought, and it is a sad thought, too, for those of us who are old."

"But, Mother, of course the stream remains unchanged," agreed Dame Adelaide. "Streams always do except after heavy rains. Everybody knows that, and I can see nothing very remarkable about it. As for you, Florian, if you stickle for love's being an immortal affair," she added, with a large twinkle, "I would have you know I have been a widow for three years. So the matter could be arranged."

Florian looked at her sadly. To him the situation was incongruous with the terrible archness of a fat woman. "But, madame, you are no longer the same person."

She patted him upon the shoulder. "Come, Florian, there is some sense in you, after all. Console yourself, lad, with the reflection that if you had stuck manfully by your wife instead of mooning about graveyards, I would still be just as I am today, and you would be tied to me. Your friend probably knew what he was about when he drank to our welfare, for we would never have suited each other, as you can see for yourself. Well, Mother, many things fall out queerly in this world, but with age we learn to accept what happens without flustering too much over it. What are we to do with this resurrected old lover of mine?"

It was horrible to Florian to see how prosaically these women dealt with his unusual misadventure. Here was a miracle occurring virtually before their eyes, and these women accepted it with maddening tranquillity as an affair for which they were not responsible. Florian began to reflect that elderly persons were always more or less unsympathetic and inadequate.

"First of all," says Dame Melicent, "I would give him some breakfast. He must be hungry after all these years. And you could put him in Adhelmar's room—"

"But," Florian said wildly, to Dame Adelaide, "you have committed the crime of bigamy, and you are, after all, my wife!"

She replied, herself not untroubled: "Yes, but, Mother, both the cook and the butler are somewhere in the bushes yonder, up to some nonsense that I prefer to know nothing about. You know how servants are, particularly on holidays. I could scramble him some eggs, though, with a rasher. And Adhelmar's room it had better be, I suppose, though I had meant to have it turned out. But as for bigamy and being your wife," she concluded more cheerfully, "it seems to me the least said the soonest mended. It is to nobody's interest to rake up those foolish bygones, so far as I can see."

"Adelaide, you profane equally love, which is divine, and marriage, which is a holy sacrament."

"Florian, do you really love Adelaide de Nointel?" asked this terrible woman. "And now that I am free to listen to your proposals, do you wish to marry me?"

"Well, no," said Florian: "for, as I have just said; you are no longer the same person."

"Why, then, you see for yourself. So do you quit talking nonsense about immortality and sacraments."

"But, still," cried Florian, "love is immortal. Yes, I repeat to you, precisely as I told Tiburce, love is immortal."

Then says Dame Melicent, nodding her shriveled old head: "When I was young, and was served by nimbler senses and desires, and was housed in brightly colored flesh, there were a host of men to love me. Minstrels yet tell of the men that loved me, and of how many tall men were slain because of their love for me, and of how in the end it was Perion who won me. For the noblest and the most faithful of all my lovers was Perion of the Forest, and through tempestuous years he sought me with a love that conquered time and chance: and so he won me. Thereafter he made me a fair husband, as husbands go. But I might not stay the girl he had loved, nor might he remain the lad that Melicent had dreamed of, with dreams be-drugging the long years in which Demetrios held Melicent a prisoner, and youth went away from her. No, Perion and I could not do that, any more than might two drops of water there retain their place in the stream's flowing. So Perion and I grew old together, friendly enough; and our senses and desires began to serve us more drowsily, so that we did not greatly mind the falling away of youth, nor greatly mind to note what shriveled hands now moved before us, performing common tasks; and we were content enough. But of the high passion that had wedded us there was no trace, and of little senseless human bickerings there were a great many. For one thing"—and the old lady's voice was changed—"for one thing, he was foolishly particular about what he would eat and what he would not eat, and that upset my housekeeping, and I had never any patience with such nonsense."

"Well, none the less," said Florian, "it is not quite nice of you to acknowledge it."

Then said Dame Adelaide: "That is a true word, Mother. All men get finicky about their food, and think they are the only persons to be considered, and there is no end to it if once you begin to humor them. So there has to be a stand made. Well, and indeed my poor Ralph, too, was all for kissing and pretty talk at first, and I accepted it willingly enough. You know how girls are. They like to be made much of, and it is perfectly natural. But that leads to children. And when the children began to come, I had not much time to bother with him: and Ralph had his farming and his warfaring to keep him busy. A man with a growing family cannot afford to neglect his affairs. And certainly, being no fool, he began to notice that girls here and there had brighter eyes and trimmer waists than I. I do not know what such observations may have led to when he was away from me: I never inquired into it, because in such matters all men are fools. But I put up with no nonsense at home, and he made me a fair husband, as husbands go. That much I will say for him gladly: and if any widow says more than that, Florian, do you beware of her, for she is an untruthful woman."

"Be that as it may," replied Florian, "it is not quite becoming to speak thus of your dead husband. No doubt you speak the truth: there is no telling what sort of person you may have married in what still seems to me unseemly haste to provide me with a successor: but even so, a little charitable prevarication would be far more edifying."

He spoke with such earnestness that there fell a silence. The women seemed to pity him. And in the silence Florian heard from afar young persons returning from the woods behind Storisende, and bringing with them the May-pole. They were still singing.

Sang they:

> *"Unwillingly foreknowing*
> *That love with May-time flees,*
> *We take this day's bestowing,*
> *And feed on fantasies—"*

4. *Youth Solves It*

THE TALE TELLS HOW LIGHTLY and sweetly, and compassionately, too, then spoke young Sylvie de Nointel.

"Ah, but, assuredly, Messire Florian, you do not argue with my pets quite seriously! Old people always have some such queer notions. Of course love all depends upon what sort of person you are. Now, as I see it, Mama and Grandmama are not the sort of persons who have real love-affairs. Devoted as I am to both of them, I cannot but perceive they are lacking in real depth of sentiment. They simply do not understand or care about such matters. They are fine, straightforward, practical persons, poor dears, and always have been, of course, for in things like that one does not change, as I have often noticed. And Father, and Grandfather Perion, too, as I remember him, was kind-hearted and admirable and all that, but nobody could ever have expected him to be a satisfactory lover. Why, he was bald as an egg, the poor pet!"

And Sylvie laughed again at the preposterous notions of old people. She flashed an especial smile at Florian. Her hand went out as though to touch him, in an unforgotten gesture. "Old people do not understand," said Sylvie de Nointel, in tones which took this handsome young fellow ineffably into confidence.

"Mademoiselle," said Florian, with a sigh that was part relief and all approval, "it is you who speak the truth, and your elders have fallen victims to the cynicism of a crassly material age. Love is immortal when it is really love and when one is the right sort of person. There is the love—known to how few, alas! and a passion of which I regret to find your mother incapable—that endures unchanged until the end of life."

"I am so glad you think so, Messire Florian," she answered demurely.

"And do you not think so, mademoiselle?"

"How should I know," she asked him, "as yet?" He noted she had incredibly long lashes.

"Thrice happy is he that convinces you!" says Florian. And about them, who were young in the world's recaptured youth, spring triumphed with an ageless rural pageant, and birds cried to their mates. He noted the red brevity of her lips and their probable softness.

Meanwhile the elder women regarded each other.

"It is the season of May. They are young and they are together. Poor children!" said Dame Melicent. "Youth cries to youth for the toys of youth, and saying, 'Lo, I cry with the voice of a great god!'"

"Still," said Madame Adelaide, "Puysange is a good fief—"

But Florian heeded neither of them as he stood there by the sunlit stream, in which no drop of water retained its place for a moment, and which yet did not alter in appearance at all. He did not heed his elders for the excellent reason that Sylvie de Nointel was about to speak, and he preferred to listen to her. For this girl, he knew, was lovelier than any other person had ever been since Eve first raised just such admiring, innocent, and venturesome eyes to inspect what must have seemed to her the quaintest of all animals, called man. So it was with a shrug that Florian remembered how he had earlier fancied other women for one reason or another; since this, he knew, was the great love of his life, and a love which would endure unchanged as long as his life lasted.

APRIL 14, 1355——OCTOBER 23, 1356

"D'aquest segle flac, plen de marrimen,
S'amor s'en vai, son jot teinh mensongier."

*S*o Florian married Sylvie, and made her, they relate, a fair husband, as husbands go. And children came to them, and then old age, and, lastly, that which comes to all.

Which reminds me that it was an uncomfortable number of years ago, in an out-of-the-way corner of the library at Allonby Shaw, that I first came upon Les Aventures d'Adhelmar de Nointel. *This manuscript dates from the early part of the fifteenth century and is attributed—though on no very conclusive evidence, says Hinsauf,—to the facile pen of Nicolas de Caen (circa 1450), until lately better known as a lyric poet and satirist.*

The story, told in decasyllabic couplets, interspersed after a rather unusual fashion with innumerable lyrics, seems in the main authentic. Sir Adhelmar de Nointel, born about 1332, was once a real and stalwart personage, a younger brother to that Henri de Nointel, the fighting Bishop of Mantes, whose unsavory part in the murder of Jacques van Arteveldt history has recorded at length; and it is with the exploits of this Adhelmar that the romance deals, not, it may be, without exaggeration.

In any event, the following is, with certain compressions and omissions that have seemed desirable, the last episode of the Aventures. *The tale concerns the children of Florian and Sylvie: and for it I may claim, at least, the same merit that old Nicolas does at the very outset; since as he veraciously declares—yet with a smack of pride:*

> *Cette bonne ystoire n'est pas usée,*
> *Ni guère de lieux jadis trouvée,*
> *Ni ècrite par clercz ne fut encore.*

II

The Episode Called Adhelmar at Puysange

I. *April-magic*

WHEN ADHELMAR HAD ENDED THE tale of Dame Venus and the love which she bore the knight Tannhäuser (here one overtakes Nicolas midcourse in narrative), Adhelmar put away the book and sighed. The Demoiselle Mélite laughed a little—her laughter, as I have told you, was high and delicate, with the resonance of thin glass—and demanded the reason of his sudden grief.

"I sigh," he answered, "for sorrow that this Dame Venus is dead."

"Surely," said she, wondering at his glum face, "that is no great matter."

"By Saint Vulfran, yes!" Adhelmar protested; "for the same Lady Venus was the fairest of women, as all learned clerks avow; and she is dead these many years, and now there is no woman left alive so beautiful as she—saving one alone, and she will have none of me. And therefore," he added, very slowly, "I sigh for desire of Dame Venus and for envy of the knight Tannhäuser."

Again Mélite laughed, but she forbore—discreetly enough—to question him concerning the lady who was of equal beauty with Dame Venus.

It was an April morning, and they set in the hedged garden of Puysange. Adhelmar read to her of divers ancient queens and of the love-business wherein each took part, relating the histories of the Lady Heleine and of her sweethearting with Duke Paris, the Emperor of Troy's son, and of the Lady Melior that loved Parthénopex of Blois, and of the Lady Aude, for love of whom Sieur Roland slew the pagan Angoulaffre, and of the Lady Cresseide that betrayed love, and of the Lady Morgaine la Fée, whose Danish lover should yet come from Avalon to save France in her black hour of need. All these he read aloud, suavely, with bland modulations, for he was a man of letters, as letters went in those days. Originally, he had been bred for the Church; but this vocation he had happily forsaken long since, protesting with some show of reason that France at this particular time had a greater need of spears than of aves.

For the rest, Sir Adhelmar de Nointel was known as a valiant knight, who had won glory in the wars with the English. He had lodged for a fortnight at Puysange, of which castle the master, Sire Reinault (son to the late Vicomte Florian) was Adhelmar's cousin: and on the next day Adhelmar proposed to set forth for Paris, where the French King—Jehan the Luckless—was gathering his lieges about him to withstand his kinsman, Edward of England.

Now, as I have said, Adhelmar was cousin to Reinault, and, in consequence, to Reinault's sister, the Demoiselle Mélite; and the latter Adhelmar loved, at least, as much as a cousin should. That was well known; and Reinault de Puysange had sworn very heartily that this was a great pity when he affianced her to Hugues d'Arques. Both Hugues and Adhelmar had loved Mélite since boyhood,—so far their claims ran equally. But while Adhelmar had busied himself in the acquisition of some scant fame and a vast number of scars, Hugues had sensibly inherited the fief of Arques, a snug property with fertile lands and a stout fortress. How, then, should Reinault hesitate between them?

He did not. For the Château d'Arques, you must understand, was builded in Lower Normandy, on the fringe of the hill-country, just where the peninsula of Cotentin juts out into the sea; Puysange stood not far north, among the level lands of Upper Normandy: and these two being the strongest castles in those parts, what more natural and desirable than that the families should be united by marriage? Reinault informed his sister of his decision; she wept a little, but did not refuse to comply.

So Adhelmar, come again to Puysange after five years' absence, found Mélite troth-plighted, fast and safe, to Hugues. Reinault told him. Adhelmar grumbled and bit his nails in a corner, for a time; then laughed shortly.

"I have loved Mélite," he said. "It may be that I love her still. Hah, Saint Vulfran! why should I not? Why should a man not love his cousin?"

Adhelmar grinned, while the vicomte twitched his beard and wished Adhelmar at the devil.

But the young knight stuck fast at Puysange, for all that, and he and Mélite were much together. Daily they made parties to dance, and to hunt the deer, and to fish, but most often to rehearse songs. For Adhelmar made good songs.*

---

* Nicolas indeed declares of Adhelmar, earlier in the tale, in such high terms as are not uncommon to this chronicle:

　　　　　JAMES BRANCH CABELL

Today, the summer already stirring in the womb of the year, they sat, as I have said, in the hedged garden; and about them the birds piped and wrangled over their nest-building, and daffodils danced in spring's honor with lively saltations, and overhead the sky was colored like a robin's egg. It was very perilous weather for young folk. By reason of this, when he had ended his reading about the lady of the hollow hill, Sir Adhelmar sighed again, and stared at his companion with hungry eyes, wherein desire strained like a hound at the leash.

Said Mélite, "Was this Lady Venus, then, exceedingly beautiful?"

Adhelmar swore an oath of sufficient magnitude that she was.

Whereupon Mélite, twisting her fingers idly and evincing a sudden interest in her own feet, demanded if this Venus were more beautiful than the Lady Ermengarde of Arnaye or the Lady Ysabeau of Brieuc.

"Holy Ouen!" scoffed Adhelmar; "these ladies, while well enough, I grant you, would seem to be callow howlets blinking about that Arabian Phoenix which Plinius tells of, in comparison with this Lady Venus that is dead!"

"But how," asked Mélite, "was this lady fashioned that you commend so highly?—and how can you know of her beauty who have never seen her?"

Said Adhelmar: "I have read of her fairness in the chronicles of Messire Stace of Thebes, and of Dares, who was her husband's bishop. And she was very comely, neither too little nor too big; she was fairer and whiter and more lovely than any flower of the lily or snow upon the branch, but her eyebrows had the mischance of meeting. She had wide-open, beautiful eyes, and her wit was quick and ready. She was graceful and of demure countenance. She was well-beloved, and could herself love well, but her heart was changeable—"

"Cousin Adhelmar," declared Mélite, flushing somewhat, for the portrait was like enough, "I think that you tell of a woman, not of a goddess of heathenry."

"Her eyes," said Adhelmar, and his voice shook, and his hands, lifting a little, trembled,—"her eyes were large and very bright and of a color like that of the June sunlight falling upon deep waters. Her hair was of a curious gold color like the Fleece that the knight Jason sought, and it

Hardi estait et fier comme lions,
Et si faisait balades et chançons,
Rondeaulx et laiz, très bans et pleins de grâce,
Comme Orpheus, cet menestrier de Thrace.

curled marvellously about her temples. For mouth she had but a small red wound; and her throat was a tower builded of ivory."

But now, still staring at her feet and glowing with the even complexion of a rose, (though not ill-pleased), the Demoiselle Mélite bade him desist and make her a song. Moreover, she added, beauty was but a fleeting thing, and she considered it of little importance; and then she laughed again.

Adhelmar took up the lute that lay beside them and fingered it for a moment, as though wondering of what he would rhyme. Afterward he sang for her as they sat in the gardens.

Sang Adhelmar:

> "It is in vain I mirror forth the praise
> In pondered virelais
> Of her that is the lady of my love;
> Far-sought and curious phrases fail to tell
> The tender miracle
> Of her white body and the grace thereof.
>
> "Thus many and many an artful-artless strain
> Is fashioned all in vain:
> Sound proves unsound; and even her name, that is
> To me more glorious than the glow of fire
> Or dawn or love's desire
> Or opals interlinked with turquoises,
> Mocks utterance.
>
> "So, lacking skill to praise
> That perfect bodily beauty which is hers,
> Even as those worshippers
> Who bore rude offerings of honey and maize,
> Their all, into the gold-paved ministers
> Of Aphrodite, I have given her these
> My faltering melodies,
> That are Love's lean and ragged messengers."

When he had ended, Adhelmar cast aside the lute, and caught up both of Mélite's hands, and strained them to his lips. There needed no wizard to read the message in his eyes.

JAMES BRANCH CABELL

Mélite sat silent for a moment. Presently, "Ah, cousin, cousin!" she sighed, "I cannot love you as you would have me love. God alone knows why, true heart, for I revere you as a strong man and a proven knight and a faithful lover; but I do not love you. There are many women who would love you, Adhelmar, for the world praises you, and you have done brave deeds and made good songs and have served your King potently; and yet"—she drew her hands away and laughed a little wearily—"yet I, poor maid, must needs love Hugues, who has done nothing. This love is a strange, unreasoning thing, my cousin."

"But do you in truth love Hugues?" asked Adhelmar, in a harsh voice.

"Yes," said Mélite, very softly, and afterward flushed and wondered dimly if she had spoken the truth. Then, somehow, her arms clasped about Adhelmar's neck, and she kissed him, from pure pity, as she told herself; for Mélite's heart was tender, and she could not endure the anguish in his face.

This was all very well. But Hugues d'Arques, coming suddenly out of a pleached walk, at this juncture, stumbled upon them and found their postures distasteful. He bent black brows upon the two.

"Adhelmar," said he, at length, "this world is a small place."

Adhelmar rose. "Indeed," he assented, with a wried smile, "I think there is scarce room in it for both of us, Hugues."

"That was my meaning," said the Sieur d'Arques.

"Only," Adhelmar pursued, somewhat wistfully, "my sword just now, Hugues, is vowed to my King's quarrel. There are some of us who hope to save France yet, if our blood may avail. In a year, God willing, I shall come again to Puysange; and till then you must wait."

Hugues conceded that, perforce, he must wait, since a vow was sacred; and Adhelmar, who suspected Hugues' natural appetite for battle to be lamentably squeamish, grinned. After that, in a sick rage, Adhelmar struck Hugues in the face, and turned about.

The Sieur d'Arques rubbed his cheek ruefully. Then he and Mélite stood silent for a moment, and heard Adhelmar in the court-yard calling his men to ride forth; and Mélite laughed; and Hugues scowled.

2. *Nicolas as Chorus*

The year passed, and Adhelmar did not return; and there was much fighting during that interval, and Hugues began to think the knight was slain and would never return to fight with him. The reflection was borne with equanimity.

So Adhelmar was half-forgot, and the Sieur d'Arques turned his mind to other matters. He was still a bachelor, for Reinault considered the burden of the times in ill-accord with the chinking of marriage-bells. They were grim times for Frenchmen: right and left the English pillaged and killed and sacked and guzzled and drank, as if they would never have done; and Edward of England began, to subscribe himself *Rex Franciae* with some show of excuse.

In Normandy men acted according to their natures. Reinault swore lustily and looked to his defences; Hugues, seeing the English everywhere triumphant, drew a long face and doubted, when the will of God was made thus apparent, were it the part of a Christian to withstand it? Then he began to write letters, but to whom no man at either Arques or Puysange knew, saving One-eyed Peire, who carried them.

3. *Treats of Huckstering*

It was in the dusk of a rain-sodden October day that Adhelmar rode to the gates of Puysange, with some score men-at-arms behind him. They came from Poictiers, where again the English had conquered, and Adhelmar rode with difficulty, for in that disastrous business in the field of Maupertuis he had been run through the chest, and his wound was scarce healed. Nevertheless, he came to finish his debate with the Sieur d'Arques, wound or no wound.

But at Puysange he heard a strange tale of Hugues. Reinault, whom Adhelmar found in a fine rage, told the story as they sat over their supper.

It had happened, somehow, (Reinault said), that the Marshal Arnold d'Andreghen—newly escaped from prison and with his disposition unameliorated by Lord Audley's gaolership,—had heard of these letters that Hugues wrote so constantly; and the Marshal, being no scholar, had frowned at such doings, and waited presently, with a company of horse, on the road to Arques. Into their midst, on the day before Adhelmar came, rode Peire, the one-eyed messenger; and it was not an unconscionable while before Peire was bound hand and foot, and d'Andreghen was reading the letter they had found in Peire's jerkin. "Hang the carrier on that oak," said d'Andreghen, when he had ended, "but leave that largest branch yonder for the writer. For by the Blood of Christ, our common salvation! I will hang him there on Monday!"

So Peire swung in the air ere long and stuck out a black tongue at the crows, who cawed and waited for supper; and presently they feasted while d'Andreghen rode to Arques, carrying a rope for Hugues.

For the Marshal, you must understand, was a man of sudden action. Only two months ago, he had taken the Comte de Harcourt with other gentlemen from the Dauphin's own table to behead them that afternoon in a field behind Rouen. It was true they had planned to resist the *gabelle*, the King's immemorial right to impose a tax on salt; but Harcourt was Hugues' cousin, and the Sieur d'Arques, being somewhat of an epicurean disposition, esteemed the dessert accorded his kinsman unpalatable.

There was no cause for great surprise to d'Andreghen, then, to find that the letter Hugues had written was meant for Edward, the Black Prince of England, now at Bordeaux, where he held the French King, whom the Prince had captured at Poictiers, as a prisoner; for this prince, though he had no particular love for a rogue, yet knew how to make use of one when kingcraft demanded it,—and, as he afterward made use of Pedro the Castilian, he was now prepared to make use of Hugues, who hung like a ripe pear ready to drop into Prince Edward's mouth. "For," as the Sieur d'Arques pointed out in his letter, "I am by nature inclined to favor you brave English, and so, beyond doubt, is the good God. And I will deliver Arques to you; and thus and thus you may take Normandy and the major portion of France; and thus and thus will I do, and thus and thus must you reward me."

Said d'Andreghen, "I will hang him at dawn; and thus and thus may the devil do with his soul!"

Then with his company d'Andreghen rode to Arques. A herald declared to the men of that place how the matter stood, and bade Hugues come forth and dance upon nothing. The Sieur d'Arques spat curses, like a cat driven into a corner, and wished to fight, but the greater part of his garrison were not willing to do so in such a cause: and so d'Andreghen took him and carried him off.

In anger having sworn by the Blood of Christ to hang Hugues d'Arques to a certain tree, d'Andreghen had no choice in calm but to abide by his oath. This day being the Sabbath, he deferred the matter; but the Marshal promised to see to it that when morning broke the Sieur d'Arques should dangle side by side with his messenger.

Thus far the Vicomte de Puysange. He concluded his narrative with a dry chuckle. "And I think we are very well rid of him, Adhelmar. Holy Maclou! that I should have taken the traitor for a true man, though! He would sell France, you observe,—chaffered, they tell me, like a pedlar over the price of Normandy. Heh, the huckster, the triple-damned Jew!"

"And Mélite?" asked Adhelmar, after a little.

Again Reinault shrugged. "In the White Turret," he said; then, with a short laugh: "Oy Dieus, yes! The girl has been caterwauling for this shabby rogue all day. She would have me—me, the King's man, look you!—save Hugues at the peril of my seignory! And I protest to you, by the most high and pious Saint Nicolas the Confessor," Reinault swore, "that sooner than see this huckster go unpunished, I would lock Hell's gate on him with my own hands!"

For a moment Adhelmar stood with his jaws puffed out, as if in thought, and then he laughed like a wolf. Afterward he went to the White Turret, leaving Reinault smiling over his wine.

4. *Folly Diversely Attested*

He found Mélite alone. She had robed herself in black, and had gathered her gold hair about her face like a heavy veil, and sat weeping into it for the plight of Hugues d'Arques.

"Mélite!" cried Adhelmar; "Mélite!" The Demoiselle de Puysange rose with a start, and, seeing him standing in the doorway, ran to him, incompetent little hands fluttering before her like frightened doves. She was very tired, by that day-long arguing with her brother's notions about honor and knightly faith and such foolish matters, and to her weariness Adhelmar seemed strength incarnate; surely he, if any one, could aid Hugues and bring him safe out of the grim marshal's claws. For the moment, perhaps, she had forgotten the feud which existed between Adhelmar and the Sieur d'Arques; but in any event, I am convinced, she knew that Adhelmar could refuse her nothing. So she ran toward him, her cheeks flushing arbutus-like, and she was smiling through her tears.

Oh, thought Adhelmar, were it not very easy to leave Hugues to the dog's death he merits and to take this woman for my own? For I know that she loves me a little. And thinking of this, he kissed her, quietly, as one might comfort a sobbing child; afterward he held her in his arms for a moment, wondering vaguely at the pliant thickness of her hair and the sweet scent of it. Then he put her from him gently, and swore in his soul that Hugues must die, so that this woman might be Adhelmar's.

"You will save him?" Mélite asked, and raised her face to his. There was that in her eyes which caused Adhelmar to muse for a little on the nature of women's love, and, subsequently, to laugh harshly and make vehement utterance.

"Yes!" said Adhelmar.

He demanded how many of Hugues' men were about. Some twenty of them had come to Puysange, Mélite said, in the hope that Reinault might aid them to save their master. She protested that her brother was a coward for not doing so; but Adhelmar, having his own opinion on this subject, and thinking in his heart that Hugues' skin might easily be ripped off him without spilling a pint of honest blood, said, simply: "Twenty and twenty is two-score. It is not a large armament, but it may serve."

He told her his plan was to fall suddenly upon d'Andreghen and his men that night, and in the tumult to steal Hugues away; whereafter, as Adhelmar pointed out, Hugues might readily take ship for England, and leave the marshal to blaspheme Fortune in Normandy, and the French King to gnaw at his chains in Bordeaux, while Hugues toasts his shins in comfort at London. Adhelmar admitted that the plan was a mad one, but added, reasonably enough, that needs must when the devil drives. And so firm was his confidence, so cheery his laugh—he managed to laugh somehow, though it was a stiff piece of work,—that Mélite began to be comforted somewhat, and bade him go and Godspeed.

So then Adhelmar left her. In the main hall he found the vicomte still sitting over his wine of Anjou.

"Cousin," said Adhelmar, "I must ride hence tonight."

Reinault stared at him: a mastering wonder woke in Reinault's face. "Ta, ta, ta!" he clicked his tongue, very softly. Afterward he sprang to his feet and clutched Adhelmar by both arms. "No, no!" Reinault cried. "No, Adhelmar, you must not try that! It is death, lad,—sure death! It means hanging, boy!" the vicomte pleaded, for, hard man that he was, he loved Adhelmar.

"That is likely enough," Adhelmar conceded.

"They will hang you," Reinault said again: "d'Andreghen and the Count Dauphin of Vienna will hang you as blithely as they would Iscariot."

"That, too," said Adhelmar, "is likely enough, if I remain in France."

"Oy Dieus! will you flee to England, then?" the vicomte scoffed, bitterly. "Has King Edward not sworn to hang you these eight years past? Was it not you, then, cousin, who took Almerigo di Pavia, that

Lombard knave whom he made governor of Calais,—was it not you, then, who delivered Edward's loved Almerigo to Geoffrey de Chargny, who had him broken on the wheel? Eh, holy Maclou! but you will get hearty welcome and a chaplain and a rope in England."

Adhelmar admitted that this was true. "Still," said he, "I must ride hence tonight."

"For her?" Reinault asked, and jerked his thumb upward.

"Yes," said Adhelmar,—"for her."

Reinault stared in his face for a while. "You are a fool, Adhelmar," said he, at last, "but you are a brave man, and you love as becomes a chevalier. It is a great pity that a flibbertigibbet wench with a tow-head should be the death of you. For my part, I am the King's vassal; I shall not break faith with him; but you are my guest and my kinsman. For that reason I am going to bed, and I shall sleep very soundly. It is likely I shall hear nothing of the night's doings,—ohimé, no! not if you murder d'Andreghen in the court-yard!" Reinault ended, and smiled, somewhat sadly.

Afterward he took Adhelmar's hand and said: "Farewell, lord Adhelmar! O true knight, sturdy and bold! terrible and merciless toward your enemies, gentle and simple toward your friends, farewell!"

He kissed Adhelmar on either cheek and left him. In those days men encountered death with very little ado.

Then Adhelmar rode off in the rain with thirty-four armed followers. Riding thus, he reflected upon the nature of women and upon his love for the Demoiselle de Puysange; and, to himself, he swore gloomily that if she had a mind to Hugues she must have Hugues, come what might. Having reached this conclusion, Adhelmar wheeled upon his men, and cursed them for tavern-idlers and laggards and flea-hearted snails, and bade them spur.

Mélite, at her window, heard them depart, and heard the noise of their going lapse into the bland monotony of the rain's noise. This dank night now divulged no more, and she turned back into the room. Adhelmar's glove, which he had forgotten in his haste, lay upon the floor, and Mélite lifted it and twisted it idly.

"I wonder—?" said she.

She lighted four wax candles and set them before a mirror that was in the room. Mélite stood among them and looked into the mirror. She seemed very tall and very slender, and her loosened hair hung heavily about her beautiful shallow face and fell like a cloak around her black-robed body, showing against the black gown like melting gold; and about her were the tall, white candles tipped with still flames of gold. Mélite laughed—her laughter was high and delicate, with the resonance of thin glass,—and raised her arms above her, head, stretching tensely like a cat before a fire, and laughed yet again.

"After all," said she, "I do not wonder."

Mélite sat before the mirror, and braided her hair, and sang to herself in a sweet, low voice, brooding with unfathomable eyes upon her image in the glass, while the October rain beat about Puysange, and Adhelmar rode forth to save Hugues that must else be hanged.

Sang Mélite:

> *"Rustling leaves of the willow-tree*
> *Peering downward at you and me,*
> *And no man else in the world to see,*

> *"Only the birds, whose dusty coats*
> *Show dark in the green,—whose throbbing throats*
> *Turn joy to music and love to notes.*

> *"Lean your body against the tree,*
> *Lifting your red lips up to me,*
> *Mélite, and kiss, with no man to see!*

> *"And let us laugh for a little:—Yea,*
> *Let love and laughter herald the day*
> *When laughter and love will be put away.*

> *"Then you will remember the willow-tree*
> *And this very hour, and remember me,*
> *Mélite,—whose face you will no more see!*

> *"So swift, so swift the glad time goes,*
> *And Eld and Death with their countless woes*
> *Draw near, and the end thereof no man knows,*

> *"Lean your body against the tree,*
> *Lifting your red lips up to me,*
> *Mélite, and kiss, with no man to see!"*

Mélite smiled as she sang; for this was a song that Adhelmar had made for her upon a May morning at Nointel, before he was a knight, when both were very young. So now she smiled to remember the making of the verses which she sang while the October rain was beating about Puysange.

5. *Night-work*

IT WAS NOT LONG BEFORE they came upon d'Andreghen and his men camped about a great oak, with One-eyed Peire a-swing over their heads for a lamentable banner. A shrill sentinel, somewhere in the dark, demanded the newcomers' business, but without receiving any adequate answer, for at that moment Adhelmar gave the word to charge.

Then it was as if all the devils in Pandemonium had chosen Normandy for their playground; and what took place in the night no man saw for the darkness, so that I cannot tell you of it. Let it suffice that Adhelmar rode away before d'Andreghen had rubbed sleep well out of his eyes; and with Adhelmar were Hugues d'Arques and some half of Adhelmar's men. The rest were dead, and Adhelmar was badly hurt, for he had burst open his old wound and it was bleeding under his armor. Of this he said nothing.

"Hugues," said he, "do you and these fellows ride to the coast; thence take ship for England."

He would have none of Hugues' thanks; instead, he turned and left Hugues to whimper out his gratitude to the skies, which spat a warm, gusty rain at him. Adhelmar rode again to Puysange, and as he went he sang.

Sang Adhelmar:

> *"D'Andreghen in Normandy*
> *Went forth to slay mine enemy;*
> *But as he went*
> *Lord God for me wrought marvellously;*
>
> *"Wherefore, I may call and cry*
> *That am now about to die,*
> *'I am content!'*
>
> *"Domine! Domine!*
> *Gratias accipe!*

Et meum animum
Recipe in coelum!"

6. They Kiss at Parting

WHEN HE HAD COME TO Puysange, Adhelmar climbed the stairs of the White Turret,—slowly, for he was growing very feeble now,—and so came again to Mélite crouching among the burned-out candles in the slate-colored twilight which heralded dawn.

"He is safe," said Adhelmar. He told Mélite how Hugues was rescued and shipped to England, and how, if she would, she might straightway follow him in a fishing-boat. "For there is likely to be ugly work at Puysange," Adhelmar said, "when the marshal comes. And he will come."

"But what will you do now, my cousin?" asked Mélite.

"Holy Ouen!" said Adhelmar; "since I needs must die, I will die in France, not in the cold land of England."

"Die!" cried Mélite. "Are you hurt so sorely, then?"

He grinned like a death's-head. "My injuries are not incurable," said he, "yet must I die very quickly, for all that. The English King will hang me if I go thither, as he has sworn to do these eight years, because of that matter of Almerigo di Pavia: and if I stay in France, I must hang because of this night's work."

Mélite wept. "O God! O God!" she quavered, two or three times, like one hurt in the throat. "And you have done this for me! Is there no way to save you, Adhelmar?" she pleaded, with wide, frightened eyes that were like a child's.

"None," said Adhelmar. He took both her hands in his, very tenderly. "Ah, my sweet," said he, "must I, whose grave is already digged, waste breath upon this idle talk of kingdoms and the squabbling men who rule them? I have but a brief while to live, and I wish to forget that there is aught else in the world save you, and that I love you. Do not weep, Mélite! In a little time you will forget me and be happy with this Hugues whom you love; and I?—ah, my sweet, I think that even in my grave I shall dream of you and of your great beauty and of the exceeding love that I bore you in the old days."

"Ah, no, I shall not ever forget, O true and faithful lover! And, indeed, indeed, Adhelmar, I would give my life right willingly that yours might be saved!"

She had almost forgotten Hugues. Her heart was sad as she thought of Adhelmar, who must die a shameful death for her sake, and of the love which she had cast away. Beside it, the Sieur d'Arques' affection showed somewhat tawdry, and Mélite began to reflect that, after all, she had liked Adhelmar almost as well.

"Sweet," said Adhelmar, "do I not know you to the marrow? You will forget me utterly, for your heart is very changeable. Ah, Mother of God!" Adhelmar cried, with a quick lift of speech; "I am afraid to die, for the harsh dust will shut out the glory of your face, and you will forget!"

"No; ah, no!" Mélite whispered, and drew near to him. Adhelmar smiled, a little wistfully, for he did not believe that she spoke the truth; but it was good to feel her body close to his, even though he was dying, and he was content.

But by this time the dawn had come completely, flooding the room with its first thin radiance, and Mélite saw the pallor of his face and so knew that he was wounded.

"Indeed, yes," said Adhelmar, when she had questioned him, "for my breast is quite cloven through." And when she disarmed him, Mélite found a great cut in his chest which had bled so much that it was apparent he must die, whether d'Andreghen and Edward of England would or no.

Mélite wept again, and cried, "Why had you not told me of this?"

"To have you heal me, perchance?" said Adhelmar. "Ah, love, is hanging, then, so sweet a death that I should choose it, rather than to die very peacefully in your arms? Indeed, I would not live if I might; for I have proven traitor to my King, and it is right that traitors should die; and, chief of all, I know that life can bring me naught more desirable than I have known this night. What need, then, have I to live?"

Mélite bent over him; for as he spoke he had lain back in a tall carven chair by the east window. She was past speech. But now, for a moment, her lips clung to his, and her warm tears fell upon his face. What better death for a lover? thought Adhelmar.

Yet he murmured somewhat. "Pity, always pity!" he said, wearily. "I shall never win aught else of you, Mélite. For before this you have kissed me, pitying me because you could not love me. And you have kissed me now, pitying me because I may not live."

But Mélite, clasping her arms about his neck, whispered into his ear the meaning of this last kiss, and at the honeyed sound of her whispering his strength came back for a moment, and he strove to rise. The level sunlight through the open window smote full upon his face, which was very glad. Mélite was conscious of her nobility in causing him such delight at the last.

"God, God!" cried Adhelmar, and he spread out his arms toward the dear, familiar world that was slowly taking form beneath them,—a world now infinitely dear to him; "all, my God, have pity and let me live a little longer!"

As Mélite, half frightened, drew back from him, he crept out of his chair and fell prone at her feet. Afterward his hands stretched forward toward her, clutching, and then trembled and were still.

Mélite stood looking downward, wondering vaguely when she would next know either joy or sorrow again. She was now conscious of no emotion whatever. It seemed to her she ought to be more greatly moved. So the new day found them.

MARCH 2, 1414

"Jack, how agrees the devil and thee about thy soul, that thou soldest him for a cup of Madeira and a cold capon's leg?"

*I*n the chapel at Puysange you may still see the tomb of Adhelmar; but Mélite's bones lie otherwhere. "Her heart was changeable," as old Nicolas says, justly enough; and so in due time it was comforted.

For Hugues d'Arques—or Hugh Darke, as his name was Anglicized—presently stood high in the favor of King Edward. A fief was granted to Messire Darke, in Norfolk, where Hugues shortly built for himself a residence at Yaxham, and began to look about for a wife: it was not long before he found one.

This befell at Brétigny when, in 1360, the Great Peace was signed between France and England, and Hugues, as one of the English embassy, came face to face with Reinault and Mélite. History does not detail the meeting; but, inasmuch as the Sieur d'Arques and Mélite de Puysange were married at Rouen the following October, doubtless it passed off pleasantly enough.

The couple had sufficient in common to have qualified them for several decades of mutual toleration. But by ill luck, Mélite died in child-birth three years after her marriage. She had borne, in 1361, twin daughters, of whom Adelais died a spinster; the other daughter, Sylvia, circa 1378, figured in an unfortunate love-affair with one of Sir Thomas Mowbray's attendants, but subsequently married Robert Vernon of Winstead. Mélite left also a son, Hugh, born in 1363, who succeeded to his father's estate of Yaxham in 1387, in which year Hugues fell at the battle of Radcot Bridge, fighting in behalf of the ill-fated Richard of Bordeaux.

Now we turn to certain happenings in Eastcheap, at the Boar's Head Tavern.

III

The Episode Called Love-Letters
of Falstaff

I. *"That Gray Iniquity"*

THERE WAS A SOUND OF scuffling within as Sir John Falstaff—much broken since his loss of the King's favor, and now equally decayed in wit and health and reputation—stood fumbling at the door of the Angel room. He was particularly shaky this morning after a night of particularly hard drinking.

But he came into the apartment singing, and, whatever the scuffling had meant, found Bardolph in one corner employed in sorting garments from a clothes-chest, while at the extreme end of the room Mistress Quickly demurely stirred the fire; which winked at the old knight rather knowingly.

"*Then came the bold Sir Caradoc*," carolled Sir John. "Ah, mistress, what news?—*And eke Sir Pellinore.*—Did I rage last night, Bardolph? Was I a Bedlamite?"

"As mine own bruises can testify," Bardolph assented. "Had each one of them a tongue, they would raise a clamor beside which Babel were as an heir weeping for his rich uncle's death; their testimony would qualify you for any mad-house in England. And if their evidence go against the doctor's stomach, the watchman at the corner hath three teeth—or, rather, hath them no longer, since you knocked them out last night—that will, right willingly, aid him to digest it."

"Three, say you?" asked the knight, rather stiffly lowering his great body into his great chair set ready for him beside the fire. "I would have my valor in all men's mouths, but not in this fashion, for it is too biting a jest. Three, say you? Well, I am glad it was no worse; I have a tender conscience, and that mad fellow of the north, Hotspur, sits heavily upon it, so that thus this Percy, being slain by my valor, is *per se* avenged, a plague on him! Three, say you? I would to God my name were not so terrible to the enemy as it is; I would I had 'bated my natural inclination somewhat, and had slain less tall fellows by some threescore. I doubt Agamemnon slept not well o' nights. Three, say you? Give the fellow a crown apiece for his mouldy teeth, if thou hast them; if thou hast them not, bid him eschew this vice of drunkenness, whereby his misfortune hath befallen him, and thus win him heavenly crowns."

"Indeed, sir," began Bardolph, "I doubt—"

"Doubt not, sirrah!" cried Sir John, testily; and continued, in a virtuous manner: "Was not the apostle reproved for that same sin? Thou art a Didymus, Bardolph;—an incredulous paynim, a most unspeculative rogue! Have I carracks trading in the Indies? Have I robbed the exchequer of late? Have I the Golden Fleece for a cloak? Nay, it is paltry gimlet, and that augurs badly. Why, does this knavish watchman take me for a raven to feed him in the wilderness? Tell him there are no such ravens hereabout; else had I ravenously limed the house-tops and set springes in the gutters. Inform him that my purse is no better lined than his own broken skull: it is void as a beggar's protestations, or a butcher's stall in Lent; light as a famished gnat, or the sighing of a new-made widower; more empty than a last year's bird-nest, than a madman's eye, or, in fine, than the friendship of a king."

"But you have wealthy friends, Sir John," suggested the hostess of the Boar's Head Tavern, whose impatience had but very hardly waited for this opportunity to join in the talk. "Yes, I warrant you, Sir John. Sir John, you have a many wealthy friends; you cannot deny that, Sir John."

"Friends, dame?" asked the knight, and cowered closer to the fire, as though he were a little cold. "I have no friends since Hal is King. I had, I grant you, a few score of acquaintances whom I taught to play at dice; paltry young blades of the City, very unfledged juvenals! Setting my knighthood and my valor aside, if I did swear friendship with these, I did swear to a lie. But this is a censorious and muddy-minded world, so that, look you, even these sprouting aldermen, these foul bacon-fed rogues, have fled my friendship of late, and my reputation hath grown somewhat more murky than Erebus. No matter! I walk alone, as one that hath the pestilence. No matter! But I grow old; I am not in the vaward of my youth, mistress."

He nodded his head with extreme gravity; then reached for a cup of sack that Bardolph held at the knight's elbow.

"Indeed, I know not what your worship will do," said Mistress Quickly, rather sadly.

"Faith!" answered Sir John, finishing the sack and grinning in a somewhat ghastly fashion; "unless the Providence that watches over the fall of a sparrow hath an eye to the career of Sir John Falstaff, Knight, and so comes to my aid shortly, I must needs convert my last doublet into a mask, and turn highwayman in my shirt. I can take purses yet, ye Uzzite comforters, as gaily as I did at Gadshill, where that scurvy Poins, and he that is now King, and some twoscore other knaves did afterward assault me in the dark; yet I peppered some of them, I warrant you!"

"You must be rid of me, then, master," Bardolph interpolated. "I for one have no need of a hempen collar."

"Ah, well!" said the knight, stretching himself in his chair as the warmth of the liquor coursed through his inert blood; "I, too, would be loth to break the gallows' back! For fear of halters, we must alter our way of living; we must live close, Bardolph, till the wars make us Croesuses or food for crows. And if Hal but hold to his bias, there will be wars: I will eat a piece of my sword, if he have not need of it shortly. Ah, go thy ways, tall Jack; there live not three good men unhanged in England, and one of them is fat and grows old. We must live close, Bardolph; we must forswear drinking and wenching! But there is lime in this sack, you rogue; give me another cup."

The old knight drained this second cup, and unctuously sucked at and licked his lips. Thereafter,

"I pray you, hostess," he continued, "remember that Doll Tearsheet sups with me tonight; have a capon of the best, and be not sparing of the wine. I will repay you, upon honor, when we young fellows return from France, all laden with rings and brooches and such trumperies like your Norfolkshire pedlars at Christmas-tide. We will sack a town for you, and bring you back the Lord Mayor's beard to stuff you a cushion; the Dauphin shall be your tapster yet; we will walk on lilies, I warrant you, to the tune of *Hey, then up go we!*"

"Indeed, sir," said Mistress Quickly, in perfect earnest, "your worship is as welcome to my pantry as the mice—a pox on 'em!—think themselves; you are heartily welcome. Ah, well, old Puss is dead; I had her of Goodman Quickly these ten years since;—but I had thought you looked for the lady who was here but now;—she was a roaring lion among the mice."

"What lady?" cried Sir John, with great animation. "Was it Flint the mercer's wife, think you? Ah, she hath a liberal disposition, and will, without the aid of Prince Houssain's carpet or the horse of Cambuscan, transfer the golden shining pieces from her husband's coffers to mine."

"No mercer's wife, I think," Mistress Quickly answered, after consideration. "She came with two patched footmen, and smacked of gentility;—Master Dumbleton's father was a mercer; but he had red hair;—she is old;—and I could never abide red hair."

"No matter!" cried the knight. "I can love this lady, be she a very Witch of Endor. Observe, what a thing it is to be a proper man, Bardolph! She hath marked me;—in public, perhaps; on the street, it may be;—and then, I warrant you, made such eyes! and sighed such sighs! and lain awake o' nights, thinking of a pleasing portly gentleman, whom, were I not modesty's self, I might name;—and I, all this while, not knowing! Fetch me my Book of Riddles and my Sonnets, that I may speak smoothly. Why was my beard not combed this morning? No matter, it will serve. Have I no better cloak than this?" Sir John was in a tremendous bustle, all a-beam with pleasurable anticipation.

But Mistress Quickly, who had been looking out of the window, said, "Come, but your worship must begin with unwashed hands, for old Madam Wish-for't and her two country louts are even now at the door."

"Avaunt, minions!" cried the knight. "Avaunt! Conduct the lady hither, hostess; Bardolph, another cup of sack. We will ruffle it, lad, and go to France all gold, like Midas! Are mine eyes too red? I must look sad, you know, and sigh very pitifully. Ah, we will ruffle it! Another cup of sack, Bardolph;—I am a rogue if I have drunk today. And avaunt! vanish! for the lady comes."

He threw himself into a gallant attitude, suggestive of one suddenly palsied, and with the mien of a turkey-cock strutted toward the door to greet his unknown visitor.

2. *"Then was Jack Falstaff, now Sir John, a Boy"*

THE WOMAN WHO ENTERED WAS not the jolly City dame one looked for: and, at first sight, you estimated her age as a trifle upon the staider side of sixty. But to this woman the years had shown unwonted kindliness, as though time touched her less with intent to mar than to caress; her form was still unbent, and her countenance, bloodless and deep-furrowed, bore the traces of great beauty; and, whatever the nature of her errand, the woman who stood in the doorway was unquestionably a person of breeding.

Sir John advanced toward her with as much elegance as he might muster; for gout when coupled with such excessive bulk does not beget an overpowering amount of grace.

"*See, from the glowing East, Aurora comes*," he chirped. "Madam, permit me to welcome you to my poor apartments; they are not worthy—"

"I would see Sir John Falstaff, sir," declared the lady, courteously, but with some reserve of manner, and looking him full in the face as she said this.

"Indeed, madam," suggested Sir John, "if those bright eyes—whose glances have already cut my poor heart into as many pieces as the man in the front of the almanac—will but desist for a moment from such butcher's work and do their proper duty, you will have little trouble in finding the bluff soldier you seek."

"Are you Sir John?" asked the lady, as though suspecting a jest. "The son of old Sir Edward Falstaff, of Norfolk?"

"His wife hath frequently assured me so," Sir John protested, very gravely; "and to confirm her evidence I have about me a certain villainous thirst that did plague Sir Edward sorely in his lifetime, and came to me with his other chattels. The property I have expended long since; but no Jew will advance me a maravedi on the Falstaff thirst. It is a priceless commodity, not to be bought or sold; you might as soon quench it."

"I would not have known you," said the lady, wonderingly; "but," she added, "I have not seen you these forty years."

"Faith, madam," grinned the knight, "the great pilferer Time hath since then taken away a little from my hair, and added somewhat (saving your presence) to my belly; and my face hath not been improved by being the grindstone for some hundred swords. But I do not know you."

"I am Sylvia Vernon," said the lady. "And once, a long while ago, I was Sylvia Darke."

"I remember," said the knight. His voice was altered. Bardolph would hardly have known it; nor, perhaps, would he have recognized his master's manner as he handed Dame Sylvia to the best chair.

"A long while ago," she repeated, sadly, after a pause during which the crackling of the fire was very audible. "Time hath dealt harshly with us both, John;—the name hath a sweet savor. I am an old woman now. And you—"

"I would not have known you," said Sir John; then asked, almost resentfully, "What do you here?"

"My son goes to the wars," she answered, "and I am come to bid him farewell; yet I should not tarry in London, for my lord is feeble and hath constant need of me. But I, an old woman, am yet vain enough to steal these few moments from him who needs me, to see for the last time, mayhap, him who was once my very dear friend."

"I was never your friend, Sylvia," said Sir John.

"Ah, the old wrangle!" said the lady, and smiled a little wistfully. "My dear and very honored lover, then; and I am come to see him here."

"Ay!" interrupted Sir John, rather hastily; and he proceeded, glowing with benevolence: "A quiet, orderly place, where I bestow my patronage; the woman of the house had once a husband in my company. God rest his soul! he bore a good pike. He retired in his old age and 'stablished this tavern, where he passed his declining years, till death called him gently away from this naughty world. God rest his soul, say I!"

This was a somewhat euphemistic version of the taking-off of Goodman Quickly, who had been knocked over the head with a joint-stool while rifling the pockets of a drunken guest; but perhaps Sir John wished to speak well of the dead, even at the price of conferring upon the present home of Sir John an idyllic atmosphere denied it by the London constabulary.

"And you for old memories' sake yet aid his widow?" the lady murmured. "That is like you, John."

There was another silence, and the fire crackled more loudly than ever.

"And are you sorry that I come again, in a worse body, John, strange and time-ruined?"

"Sorry?" echoed Sir John; and, ungallant as it was, he hesitated a moment before replying: "No, faith! But there are some ghosts that will not easily bear raising, and you have raised one."

"We have summoned up no very fearful spectre, I think," replied the lady; "at most, no worse than a pallid, gentle spirit that speaks—to me, at least—of a boy and a girl who loved each other and were very happy a great while ago."

"Are you come hither to seek that boy?" asked the knight, and chuckled, though not merrily. "The boy that went mad and rhymed of you in those far-off dusty years? He is quite dead, my lady; he was drowned, mayhap, in a cup of wine. Or he was slain, perchance, by a few light women. I know not how he died. But he is quite dead, my lady, and I had not been haunted by his ghost until today."

He stared at the floor as he ended; then choked, and broke into a fit of coughing which unromantic chance brought on just now, of all times.

"He was a dear boy," she said, presently; "a boy who loved a young maid very truly; a boy that found the maid's father too strong and shrewd for desperate young lovers—Eh, how long ago it seems, and what a flood of tears the poor maid shed at being parted from that dear boy!"

"Faith!" admitted Sir John, "the rogue had his good points."

"Ah, John, you have not forgotten, I know," the lady said, looking up into his face, "and, you will believe me that I am very heartily sorry for the pain I brought into your life?"

"My wounds heal easily," said Sir John.

"For though my dear dead father was too wise for us, and knew it was for the best that I should not accept your love, believe me, John, I always knew the value of that love, and have held it an honor that any woman must prize."

"Dear lady," the knight suggested, with a slight grimace, "the world is not altogether of your opinion."

"I know not of the world," she said; "for we live away from it. But we have heard of you ever and anon; I have your life quite letter-perfect for these forty years or more."

"You have heard of me?" asked Sir John; and, for a seasoned knave, he looked rather uncomfortable.

"As a gallant and brave soldier," she answered; "of how you fought at sea with Mowbray that was afterward Duke of Norfolk; of your knighthood by King Richard; of how you slew the Percy at Shrewsbury; and captured Coleville o' late in Yorkshire; and how the Prince, that now is King, did love you above all men; and, in fine, of many splendid doings in the great world."

Sir John raised a protesting hand. He said, with commendable modesty: "I have fought somewhat. But we are not Bevis of Southampton; we have slain no giants. Heard you naught else?"

"Little else of note," replied the lady; and went on, very quietly: "But we are proud of you at home in Norfolk. And such tales as I have heard I have woven together in one story; and I have told it many times to my children as we sat on the old Chapel steps at evening, and the shadows lengthened across the lawn, and I bid them emulate this, the most perfect knight and gallant gentleman that I have known. And they love you, I think, though but by repute."

Once more silence fell between them; and the fire grinned wickedly at the mimic fire reflected by the old chest, as though it knew of a most entertaining secret.

"Do you yet live at Winstead?" asked Sir John, half idly.

"Yes," she answered; "in the old house. It is little changed, but there are many changes about."

"Is Moll yet with you that did once carry our letters?"

"Married to Hodge, the tanner," the lady said; "and dead long since."

"And all our merry company?" Sir John demanded. "Marian? And Tom and little Osric? And Phyllis? And Adelais? Zounds, it is like a breath of country air to speak their names once more."

"All dead," she answered, in a hushed voice, "save Adelais, and even to me poor Adelais seems old and strange. Walter was slain in the French wars, and she hath never married."

"All dead," Sir John informed the fire, as if confidentially; then he laughed, though his bloodshot eyes were not merry. "This same Death hath a wide maw! It is not long before you and I, my lady, will be at supper with the worms. But you, at least, have had a happy life."

"I have been content enough," she said, "but all that seems run by; for, John, I think that at our age we are not any longer very happy nor very miserable."

"Faith!" agreed Sir John, "we are both old; and I had not known it, my lady, until today."

Again there was silence; and again the fire leapt with delight at the jest.

Sylvia Vernon arose suddenly and cried, "I would I had not come!"

Then said Sir John: "Nay, this is but a feeble grieving you have wakened. For, madam—you whom I loved once!—you are in the right. Our blood runs thinner than of yore; and we may no longer, I think, either sorrow or rejoice very deeply."

"It is true," she said; "but I must go; and, indeed, I would to God I had not come!"

Sir John was silent; he bowed his head, in acquiescence perhaps, in meditation it may have been; but he stayed silent.

"Yet," said she, "there is something here which I must keep no longer: for here are all the letters you ever writ me."

Whereupon she handed Sir John a little packet of very old and very faded papers. He turned them awkwardly in his hand once or twice; then stared at them; then at the lady.

"You have kept them—always?" he cried.

"Yes," she responded, wistfully; "but I must not be guilty of continuing such follies. It is a villainous example to my grandchildren," Dame Sylvia told him, and smiled. "Farewell."

Sir John drew close to her and took her hands in his. He looked into her eyes for an instant, holding himself very erect,—and it was a rare event when Sir John looked any one squarely in the eyes,—and he said, wonderingly, "How I loved you!"

"I know," she murmured. Sylvia Vernon gazed up into his bloated old face with a proud tenderness that was half-regretful. A quavering came into her gentle voice. "And I thank you for your gift, my lover,—O brave true lover, whose love I was not ever ashamed to own! Farewell, my dear; yet a little while, and I go to seek the boy and girl we know of."

"I shall not be long, madam," said Sir John. "Speak a kind word for me in Heaven; for I shall have sore need of it."

She had reached the door by this. "You are not sorry that I came?"

Sir John answered, very sadly: "There are many wrinkles now in your dear face, my lady; the great eyes are a little dimmed, and the sweet laughter is a little cracked; but I am not sorry to have seen you thus. For I have loved no woman truly save you alone; and I am not sorry. Farewell." And for a moment he bowed his unreverend gray head over her shrivelled fingers.

3. "*This Pitch, as Ancient Writers do Report, doth Defile*"

"Lord, Lord, how subject we old men are to the vice of lying!" chuckled Sir John, and leaned back rheumatically in his chair and mumbled over the jest.

"Yet it was not all a lie," he confided, as if in perplexity, to the fire; "but what a coil over a youthful green-sickness 'twixt a lad and a wench more than forty years syne!

"I might have had money of her for the asking," he presently went on; "yet I am glad I did not; which is a parlous sign and smacks of dotage."

He nodded very gravely over this new and alarming phase of his character.

"Were it not a quaint conceit, a merry tickle-brain of Fate," he asked of the leaping flames, after a still longer pause, "that this mountain of malmsey were once a delicate stripling with apple cheeks and a clean breath, smelling of civet, and as mad for love, I warrant you, as any Amadis of them all? For, if a man were to speak truly, I did love her.

"I had the special marks of the pestilence," he assured a particularly incredulous—and obstinate-looking coal,—a grim, black fellow that, lurking in a corner, scowled forbiddingly and seemed to defy both the flames and Sir John. "Not all the flagons and apples in the universe might have comforted me; I was wont to sigh like a leaky bellows; to weep like a wench that hath lost her grandam; to lard my speech with the fag-ends of ballads like a man milliner; and did, indeed, indite sonnets, canzonets, and what not of mine own elaboration.

"And Moll did carry them," he continued; "plump brown-eyed Moll, that hath married Hodge the tanner, and reared her tannerkins, and died long since."

But the coal remained incredulous, and the flames crackled merrily.

"Lord, Lord, what did I not write?" said Sir John, drawing out a paper from the packet, and deciphering by the firelight the faded writing.

Read Sir John:

> *"Have pity, Sylvia? Cringing at thy door*
> *Entreats with dolorous cry and clamoring,*
> *That mendicant who quits thee nevermore;*
> *Now winter chills the world, and no birds sing*
> *In any woods, yet as in wanton Spring*
> *He follows thee; and never will have done,*
> *Though nakedly he die, from following*
> *Whither thou leadest.*
>
> *"Canst thou look upon*
> *His woes, and laugh to see a goddess' son*
> *Of wide dominion, and in strategy*
>
> *"More strong than Jove, more wise than Solomon,*
> *Inept to combat thy severity?*
> *Have pity, Sylvia! And let Love be one*
> *Among the folk that bear thee company."*

"Is it not the very puling speech of your true lover?" he chuckled; and the flames spluttered assent. *"Among the folk that bear thee company,"* he repeated, and afterward looked about him with a smack of gravity. "Faith, Adam Cupid hath forsworn my fellowship long since; he hath no score chalked up against him at the Boar's Head Tavern; or, if he have, I doubt not the next street-beggar might discharge it."

"And she hath commended me to her children as a very gallant gentleman and a true knight," Sir John went on, reflectively. He cast his eyes toward the ceiling, and grinned at invisible deities. "Jove that sees all hath a goodly commodity of mirth; I doubt not his sides ache at times, as if they had conceived another wine-god."

"Yet, by my honor," he insisted to the fire; then added, apologetically,— "if I had any, which, to speak plain, I have not,—I am glad; it is a brave jest; and I did love her once."

Then the time-battered, bloat rogue picked out another paper, and read:

My dear lady,
    That I am not with thee tonight is, indeed, no fault of mine; for Sir Thomas Mowbray hath need of me, he saith. Yet the service that I have rendered him thus far is but to cool my heels in his antechamber and dream of two great eyes and of that net of golden hair wherewith Lord Love hath lately snared my poor heart. For it comforts me—' *And so on, and so on, the pen trailing most juvenal sugar, like a fly newly crept out of the honey-pot. And ending with a posy, filched, I warrant you, from some ring.*

"I remember when I did write her this," he explained to the fire. "Lord, Lord, if the fire of grace were not quite out of me, now should I be moved. For I did write it; and it was sent with a sonnet, all of Hell, and Heaven, and your pagan gods, and other tricks of speech. It should be somewhere."

He fumbled with uncertain fingers among the papers. "Ah, here it is," he said at last, and he again began to read aloud.

Read Sir John:

> *"Cupid invaded Hell, and boldly drove*
> *Before him all the hosts of Erebus,*
> *Till he had conquered: and grim Cerberus*
> *Sang madrigals, the Furies rhymed of love,*
> *Old Charon sighed, and sonnets rang above*
> *The gloomy Styx; and even as Tantalus*
> *Was Proserpine discrowned in Tartarus,*
> *And Cupid regnant in the place thereof.*

"Thus Love is monarch throughout Hell today;
In Heaven we know his power was always great;
And Earth acclaimed Love's mastery straightway
When Sylvia came to gladden Earth's estate:—
Thus Hell and Heaven and Earth his rule obey,
And Sylvia's heart alone is obdurate.

"Well, well," sighed Sir John, "it was a goodly rogue that writ it, though the verse runs but lamely! A goodly rogue!

"He might," Sir John suggested, tentatively, "have lived cleanly, and forsworn sack; he might have been a gallant gentleman, and begotten grandchildren, and had a quiet nook at the ingleside to rest his old bones: but he is dead long since. He might have writ himself *armigero* in many a bill, or obligation, or quittance, or what not; he might have left something behind him save unpaid tavern bills; he might have heard cases, harried poachers, and quoted old saws; and slept in his own family chapel through sermons yet unwrit, beneath his presentment, done in stone, and a comforting bit of Latin: but he is dead long since."

Sir John sat meditating for a while; it had grown quite dark in the room as he muttered to himself. He rose now, rather cumbrously and uncertainly, but with a fine rousing snort of indignation.

"Zooks!" he said, "I prate like a death's-head. A thing done hath an end, God have mercy on us all! And I will read no more of the rubbish."

He cast the packet into the heart of the fire; the yellow papers curled at the edges, rustled a little, and blazed; he watched them burn to the last spark.

"A cup of sack to purge the brain!" cried Sir John, and filled one to the brim. "And I will go sup with Doll Tearsheet."

"Anoon her herte hath pitee of his wo,
And with that pitee, love com in also;
Thus is this quene in pleasaunce and in loye."

*M*eanwhile had old Dome Sylvia returned contentedly to the helpmate whom she had accepted under compulsion, and who had made her a fair husband, as husbands go. It is duly recorded, indeed, on their shared tomb, that their forty years of married life were of continuous felicity, and set a pattern to all Norfolk. The more prosaic verbal tradition is that Lady Vernon retained Sir Robert well in hand by pointing out, at judicious intervals, that she had only herself to blame for having married such a selfish person in preference to a hero of the age and an ornament of the loftiest circles.

I find, on consultation of the Allonby records, that Sylvia Vernon died of a quinsy, in 1419, surviving Sir Robert by some three months. She had borne him four sons and four daughters: of these there remained at Winstead in 1422 only Sir Hugh Vernon, the oldest son, knighted by Henry V at Agincourt, where Vernon had fought with distinction; and Adelais Vernon, the youngest daughter, with whom the following has to do.

IV

The Episode Called "Sweet Adelais"

1. *Gruntings at Aeaea*

IT WAS ON A CLEAR September day that the Marquis of Falmouth set
out for France. John of Bedford had summoned him posthaste when
Henry V was stricken at Senlis with what bid fair to prove a mortal
distemper; for the marquis was Bedford's comrade-in-arms, veteran of
Shrewsbury, Agincourt and other martial disputations, and the Duke-
Regent suspected that, to hold France in case of the King's death, he
would presently need all the help he could muster.

"And I, too, look for warm work," the marquis conceded to Mistress
Adelais Vernon, at parting. "But, God willing, my sweet, we shall be
wed at Christmas for all that. The Channel is not very wide. At a pinch
I might swim it, I think, to come to you."

He kissed her and rode away with his men. Adelais stared after
them, striving to picture her betrothed rivalling Leander in this
fashion, and subsequently laughed. The marquis was a great lord
and a brave captain, but long past his first youth; his actions went
somewhat too deliberately ever to be roused to the high lunacies
of the Sestian amorist. So Adelais laughed, but a moment later,
recollecting the man's cold desire of her, his iron fervors, Adelais
shuddered.

This was in the court-yard at Winstead. Roger Darke of
Yaxham, the girl's cousin, standing beside her, noted the gesture, and
snarled.

"Think twice of it, Adelais," said he.

Whereupon Mistress Vernon flushed like a peony. "I honor him,"
she said, with some irrelevance, "and he loves me."

Roger scoffed. "Love, love! O you piece of ice! You gray-stone
saint! What do you know of love?" Master Darke caught both her
hands in his. "Now, by Almighty God, our Saviour and Redeemer,
Jesus Christ!" he said, between his teeth, his eyes flaming; "I, Roger
Darke, have offered you undefiled love and you have mocked at it.
Ha, Tears of Mary! how I love you! And you mean to marry this

man for his title! Do you not believe that I love you, Adelais?" he whimpered.

Gently she disengaged herself. This was of a pattern with Roger's behavior any time during the past two years. "I suppose you do," Adelais conceded, with the tiniest possible shrug. "Perhaps that is why I find you so insufferable."

Afterward Mistress Vernon turned on her heel and left Master Darke. In his fluent invocation of Mahound and Termagaunt and other overseers of the damned he presently touched upon eloquence.

2. *Comes One with Moly*

ADELAIS CAME INTO THE WALLED garden of Winstead, aflame now with autumnal scarlet and gold. She seated herself upon a semicircular marble bench, and laughed for no apparent reason, and contentedly waited what Dame Luck might send.

She was a comely maid, past argument or (as her lovers habitually complained) any adequate description. Circe, Colchian Medea, Viviane du Lac, were their favorite analogues; and what old romancers had fabled concerning these ladies they took to be the shadow of which Adelais Vernon was the substance. At times these rhapsodists might have supported their contention with a certain speciousness, such as was apparent today, for example, when against the garden's hurly-burly of color, the prodigal blazes of scarlet and saffron and wine-yellow, the girl's green gown glowed like an emerald, and her eyes, too, seemed emeralds, vivid, inscrutable, of a clear verdancy that was quite untinged with either blue or gray. Very black lashes shaded them. The long oval of her face (you might have objected), was of an absolute pallor, rarely quickening to a flush; but her petulant lips burned crimson, and her hair mimicked the dwindling radiance of the autumn sunlight and shamed it. All in all, the aspect of Adelais Vernon was, beyond any questioning, spiced with a sorcerous tang; say, the look of a young witch shrewd at love-potions, but ignorant of their flavor; yet before this the girl's comeliness had stirred men's hearts to madness, and the county boasted of it.

Presently Adelais lifted her small imperious head, and then again she smiled, for out of the depths of the garden, with an embellishment of divers trills and roulades, came a man's voice that carolled blithely.

Sang the voice:

"Had you lived when earth was new
What had bards of old to do
Save to sing in praise of you?

"Had you lived in ancient days,
Adelais, sweet Adelais,
You had all the ancients' praise,—
You whose beauty would have won
Canticles of Solomon,
Had the sage Judean king
Gazed upon this goodliest thing
Earth of Heaven's grace hath got.

"Had you gladdened Greece, were not
All the nymphs of Greece forgot?

"Had you trod Sicilian ways,
Adelais, sweet Adelais,

"You had pilfered all their praise:
Bion and Theocritus
Had transmitted unto us
Honeyed harmonies to tell
Of your beauty's miracle,
Delicate, desirable,
And their singing skill were bent
You-ward tenderly,—content,
While the world slipped by, to gaze
On the grace of you, and praise
Sweet Adelais."

Here the song ended, and a man, wheeling about the hedge, paused to regard her with adoring eyes. Adelais looked up at him, incredibly surprised by his coming.

This was the young Sieur d'Arnaye, Hugh Vernon's prisoner, taken at Agincourt seven years earlier and held since then, by the King's command, without ransom; for it was Henry's policy to release none of the important French prisoners. Even on his death-bed he found time to admonish his brother, John of Bedford, that four of these,—

Charles d'Orleans and Jehan de Bourbon and Arthur de Rougemont and Fulke d'Arnaye,—should never be set at liberty. "Lest," as the King said, with a savor of prophecy, "more fire be kindled in one day than all your endeavors can quench in three."

Presently the Sieur d'Arnaye sighed, rather ostentatiously; and Adelais laughed, and demanded the cause of his grief.

"Mademoiselle," he said,—his English had but a trace of accent,—"I am afflicted with a very grave malady."

"What is the name of this malady?" said she.

"They call it love, mademoiselle."

Adelais laughed yet again and doubted if the disease were incurable. But Fulke d'Arnaye seated himself beside her and demonstrated that, in his case, it might not ever be healed.

"For it is true," he observed, "that the ancient Scythians, who lived before the moon was made, were wont to cure this distemper by blood-letting under the ears; but your brother, mademoiselle, denies me access to all knives. And the leech Aelian avers that it may be cured by the herb agnea; but your brother, mademoiselle, will not permit that I go into the fields in search of this herb. And in Greece—he, mademoiselle, I might easily be healed of my malady in Greece! For in Greece is the rock, Leucata Petra, from which a lover may leap and be cured; and the well of the Cyziceni, from which a lover may drink and be cured; and the river Selemnus, in which a lover may bathe and be cured: but your brother will not permit that I go to Greece. You have a very cruel brother, mademoiselle; seven long years, no less, he has penned me here like a starling in a cage."

And Fulke d'Arnaye shook his head at her reproachfully.

Afterward he laughed. Always this Frenchman found something at which to laugh; Adelais could not remember in all the seven years a time when she had seen him downcast. But while his lips jested of his imprisonment, his eyes stared at her mirthlessly, like a dog at his master, and her gaze fell before the candor of the passion she saw in them.

"My lord," said Adelais, "why will you not give your parole? Then you would be free to come and go as you elected." A little she bent toward him, a covert red showing in her cheeks. "Tonight at Halvergate the Earl of Brudenel holds the feast of Saint Michael. Give your parole, my lord, and come with us. There will be in our company fair ladies who may perhaps heal your malady."

But the Sieur d'Arnaye only laughed. "I cannot give my parole," he said, "since I mean to escape for all your brother's care." Then he fell to pacing up and down before her. "Now, by Monseigneur Saint Médard and the Eagle that sheltered him!" he cried, in half-humorous self-mockery; "however thickly troubles rain upon me, I think that I shall never give up hoping!" After a pause, "Listen, mademoiselle," he went on, more gravely, and gave a nervous gesture toward the east, "yonder is France, sacked, pillaged, ruinous, prostrate, naked to her enemy. But at Vincennes, men say, the butcher of Agincourt is dying. With him dies the English power in France. Can his son hold that dear realm? Are those tiny hands with which this child may not yet feed himself capable to wield a sceptre? Can he who is yet beholden to nurses for milk distribute sustenance to the law and justice of a nation? He, I think not, mademoiselle! France will have need of me shortly. Therefore, I cannot give my parole."

"Then must my brother still lose his sleep, lord, for always your safe-keeping is in his mind. Today at cock-crow he set out for the coast to examine those Frenchmen who landed yesterday."

At this he wheeled about. "Frenchmen!"

"Only Norman fishermen, lord, whom the storm drove to seek shelter in England. But he feared they had come to rescue you."

Fulke d'Arnaye shrugged his shoulders. "That was my thought, too," he admitted, with a laugh. "Always I dream of escape, mademoiselle. Have a care of me, sweet enemy! I shall escape yet, it may be."

"But I will not have you escape," said Adelais. She tossed her glittering little head. "Winstead would not be Winstead without you. Why, I was but a child, my lord, when you came. Have you forgotten, then, the lank, awkward child who used to stare at you so gravely?"

"Mademoiselle," he returned, and now his voice trembled and still the hunger in his eyes grew more great, "I think that in all these years I have forgotten nothing—not even the most trivial happening, mademoiselle,—wherein you had a part. You were a very beautiful child. Look you, I remember as if it were yesterday that you never wept when your good lady mother—whose soul may Christ have in his keeping!— was forced to punish you for some little misdeed. No, you never wept; but your eyes would grow wistful, and you would come to me here in the garden, and sit with me for a long time in silence. 'Fulke,' you would say, quite suddenly, 'I love you better than my mother.' And I told you that it was wrong to make such observations, did I not, mademoiselle?

My faith, yes! but I may confess now that I liked it," Fulke d'Arnaye ended, with a faint chuckle.

Adelais sat motionless. Certainly it was strange, she thought, how the sound of this man's voice had power to move her. Certainly, too, this man was very foolish.

"And now the child is a woman,—a woman who will presently be Marchioness of Falmouth. Look you, when I get free of my prison— and I shall get free, never fear, mademoiselle,—I shall often think of that great lady. For only God can curb a man's dreams, and God is compassionate. So I hope to dream nightly of a gracious lady whose hair is gold and whose eyes are colored like the summer sea and whose voice is clear and low and very wonderfully sweet. Nightly, I think, the vision of that dear enemy will hearten me to fight for France by day. In effect, mademoiselle, your traitor beauty will yet aid me to destroy your country."

The Sieur d'Arnaye laughed, somewhat cheerlessly, as he lifted her hand to his lips.

And certainly also (she concluded her reflections) it was absurd how this man's touch seemed an alarm to her pulses. Adelais drew away from him.

"No!" she said: "remember, lord, I, too, am not free."

"Indeed, we tread on dangerous ground," the Frenchman assented, with a sad little smile. "Pardon me, mademoiselle. Even were you free of your trothplight—even were I free of my prison, most beautiful lady, I have naught to offer you yonder in that fair land of France. They tell me that the owl and the wolf hunt undisturbed where Arnaye once stood. My château is carpeted with furze and roofed with God's Heaven. That gives me a large estate—does it not?—but I may not reasonably ask a woman to share it. So I pray you pardon me for my nonsense, mademoiselle, and I pray that the Marchioness of Falmouth may be very happy."

And with that he vanished into the autumn-fired recesses of the garden, singing, his head borne stiff. Oh, the brave man who esteemed misfortune so slightly! thought Adelais. She remembered that the Marquis of Falmouth rarely smiled; and once only—at a bull-baiting— had she heard him laugh. It needed bloodshed, then, to amuse him, Adelais deduced, with that self-certainty in logic which is proper to youth; and the girl shuddered.

But through the scarlet coppices of the garden, growing fainter and yet more faint, rang the singing of Fulke d'Arnaye.

Sang the Frenchman:

> *"Had you lived in Roman times*
> *No Catullus in his rhymes*
> *Had lamented Lesbia's sparrow:*
> *He had praised your forehead, narrow*
> *As the newly-crescent moon,*
> *White as apple-trees in June;*
> *He had made some amorous tune*
> *Of the laughing light Eros*
> *Snared as Psyche-ward he goes*
> *By your beauty,—by your slim,*
> *White, perfect beauty.*

> *"After him*
> *Horace, finding in your eyes*
> *Horace limned in lustrous wise,*
> *Would have made you melodies*
> *Fittingly to hymn your praise,*
> *Sweet Adelais."*

3. Roger is Explicit

INTO THE MIDST OF THE Michaelmas festivities at Halvergate that night, burst a mud-splattered fellow in search of Sir Hugh Vernon. Roger Darke brought him to the knight. The fellow then related that he came from Simeon de Beck, the master of Castle Rising, with tidings that a strange boat, French-rigged, was hovering about the north coast. Let Sir Hugh have a care of his prisoner.

Vernon swore roundly. "I must look into this," he said. "But what shall I do with Adelais?"

"Will you not trust her to me?" Roger asked. "If so, cousin, I will very gladly be her escort to Winstead. Let the girl dance her fill while she may, Hugh. She will have little heart for dancing after a month or so of Falmouth's company."

"That is true," Vernon assented; "but the match is a good one, and she is bent upon it."

So presently he rode with his men to the north coast. An hour later Roger Darke and Adelais set out for Winstead, in spite of all Lady

Brudenel's protestations that Mistress Vernon had best lie with her that night at Halvergate.

It was a clear night of restless winds, neither warm nor chill, but fine September weather. About them the air was heavy with the damp odors of decaying leaves, for the road they followed was shut in by the autumn woods, that now arched the way with sere foliage, rustling and whirring and thinly complaining overhead, and now left it open to broad splashes of moonlight, where fallen leaves scuttled about in the wind vortices. Adelais, elate with dancing, chattered of this and that as her gray mare ambled homeward, but Roger was moody.

Past Upton the road branched in three directions; here Master Darke caught the gray mare's bridle and turned both horses to the left.

"Why, of whatever are you thinking!" the girl derided him. "Roger, this is not the road to Winstead!"

He grinned evilly over his shoulder. "It is the road to Yaxham, Adelais, where my chaplain expects us."

In a flash she saw it all as her eyes swept these desolate woods. "You will not dare!"

"Will I not?" said Roger. "Faith, for my part, I think you have mocked me for the last time, Adelais, since it is the wife's duty, as Paul very justly says, to obey."

Swiftly she slipped from the mare. But he followed her. "Oh, infamy!" the girl cried. "You have planned this, you coward!"

"Yes, I planned it," said Roger Darke. "Yet I take no great credit therefor, for it was simple enough. I had but to send a feigned message to your block-head brother. Ha, yes, I planned it, Adelais, and I planned it well. But I deal honorably. Tomorrow you will be Mistress Darke, never fear."

He grasped at her cloak as she shrank from him. The garment fell, leaving the girl momentarily free, her festival jewels shimmering in the moonlight, her bared shoulders glistening like silver. Darke, staring at her, giggled horribly. An instant later Adelais fell upon her knees.

"Sweet Christ, have pity upon Thy handmaiden! Do not forsake me, sweet Christ, in my extremity! Save me from this man!" she prayed, with entire faith.

"My lady wife," said Darke, and his hot, wet hand sank heavily upon her shoulder, "you had best finish your prayer before my chaplain, I think, since by ordinary Holy Church is skilled to comfort the sorrowing."

　　　　　　　　　　　　　　　　JAMES BRANCH CABELL

"A miracle, dear lord Christ!" the girl wailed. "O sweet Christ, a miracle!"

"Faith of God!" said Roger, in a flattish tone; "what was that?"

For faintly there came the sound of one singing.

Sang the distant voice:

> *"Had your father's household been*
> *Guelfic-born or Ghibelline,*
> *Beatrice were unknown*
> *On her star-encompassed throne.*

> *"For, had Dante viewed your grace,*
> *Adelais, sweet Adelais,*
> *You had reigned in Bice's place,—*
> *Had for candles, Hyades,*
> *Rastaben, and Betelguese,—*
> *And had heard Zachariel*
> *Chaunt of you, and, chaunting, tell*
> *All the grace of you, and praise*
> *Sweet Adelais."*

4. *Honor Brings a Padlock*

ADELAIS SPRANG TO HER FEET. "A miracle!" she cried, her voice shaking. "Fulke, Fulke! to me, Fulke!"

Master Darke hurried her struggling toward his horse. Darke was muttering curses, for there was now a beat of hoofs in the road yonder that led to Winstead. "Fulke, Fulke!" the girl shrieked.

Then presently, as Roger put foot to stirrup, two horsemen wheeled about the bend in the road, and one of them leapt to the ground.

"Mademoiselle," said Fulke d'Arnaye, "am I, indeed, so fortunate as to be of any service to you?"

"Ho!" cried Roger, with a gulp of relief, "it is only the French dancing-master taking French leave of poor cousin Hugh! Man, but you startled me!"

Now Adelais ran to the Frenchman, clinging to him the while that she told of Roger's tricks. And d'Arnaye's face set mask-like.

"Monsieur," he said, when she had ended, "you have wronged a sweet and innocent lady. As God lives, you shall answer to me for this."

"Look you," Roger pointed out, "this is none of your affair, Monsieur Jackanapes. You are bound for the coast, I take it. Very well,—ka me, and I ka thee. Do you go your way in peace, and let us do the same."

Fulke d'Arnaye put the girl aside and spoke rapidly in French to his companion. Then with mincing agility he stepped toward Master Darke.

Roger blustered. "You hop-toad! you jumping-jack!" said he, "what do you mean?"

"Chastisement!" said the Frenchman, and struck him in the face.

"Very well!" said Master Darke, strangely quiet. And with that they both drew.

The Frenchman laughed, high and shrill, as they closed, and afterward he began to pour forth a voluble flow of discourse. Battle was wine to the man.

"Not since Agincourt, Master Coward—he, no!—have I held sword in hand. It is a good sword, this,—a sharp sword, is it not? Ah, the poor arm—but see, your blood is quite black-looking in this moonlight, and I had thought cowards yielded a paler blood than brave men possess. We live and learn, is it not? Observe, I play with you like a child,—as I played with your tall King at Agincourt when I cut away the coronet from his helmet. I did not kill him—no!—but I wounded him, you conceive? Presently, I shall wound you, too. My compliments—you have grazed my hand. But I shall not kill you, because you are the kinsman of the fairest lady earth may boast, and I would not willingly shed the least drop of any blood that is partly hers. Ohé, no! Yet since I needs must do this ungallant thing—why, see, monsieur, how easy it is!"

Thereupon he cut Roger down at a blow and composedly set to wiping his sword on the grass. The Englishman lay like a log where he had fallen.

"Lord," Adelais quavered, "lord, have you killed him?"

Fulke d'Arnaye sighed. "Hélas, no!" said he, "since I knew that you did not wish it. See, mademoiselle,—I have but made a healthful and blood-letting small hole in him here. He will return himself to survive to it long time—Fie, but my English fails me, after these so many years—"

D'Arnaye stood for a moment as if in thought, concluding his meditations with a grimace. After that he began again to speak in French to his companion. The debate seemed vital. The stranger gesticulated, pleaded, swore, implored, summoned all inventions between the starry spheres and the mud of Cocytus to judge of the affair; but Fulke d'Arnaye was resolute.

"Behold, mademoiselle," he said, at length, "how my poor Olivier excites himself over a little matter. Olivier is my brother, most beautiful lady, but he speaks no English, so that I cannot present him to you. He came to rescue me, this poor Olivier, you conceive. Those Norman fishermen of whom you spoke today—but you English are blinded, I think, by the fogs of your cold island. Eight of the bravest gentlemen in France, mademoiselle, were those same fishermen, come to bribe my gaoler,—the incorruptible Tompkins, no less. Hé, yes, they came to tell me that Henry of Monmouth, by the wrath of God King of France, is dead at Vincennes yonder, mademoiselle, and that France will soon be free of you English. France rises in her might—" His nostrils dilated, he seemed taller; then he shrugged. "And poor Olivier grieves that I may not strike a blow for her,—grieves that I must go back to Winstead."

D'Arnaye laughed as he caught the bridle of the gray mare and turned her so that Adelais might mount. But the girl, with a faint, wondering cry, drew away from him.

"You will go back! You have escaped, lord, and you will go back!"

"Why, look you," said the Frenchman, "what else may I conceivably do? We are some miles from your home, most beautiful lady,—can you ride those four long miles alone? in this night so dangerous? Can I leave you here alone in this so tall forest? Hé, surely not. I am desolated, mademoiselle, but I needs must burden you with my company homeward."

Adelais drew a choking breath. He had fretted out seven years of captivity. Now he was free; and lest she be harmed or her name be smutched, however faintly, he would go back to his prison, jesting. "No, no!" she cried aloud.

But he raised a deprecating hand. "You cannot go alone. Olivier here would go with you gladly. Not one of those brave gentlemen who await me at the coast yonder but would go with you very, very gladly, for they love France, these brave gentlemen, and they think that I can serve her better than most other men. That is very flattering, is it not? But all the world conspires to flatter me, mademoiselle. Your good brother, by example, prizes my company so highly that he would infallibly hang the gentleman who rode back with you. So, you conceive, I cannot avail myself of their services. But with me it is different, hein? Ah, yes, Sir

Hugh will merely lock me up again and for the future guard me more vigilantly. Will you not mount, mademoiselle?"

His voice was quiet, and his smile never failed him. It was this steady smile which set her heart to aching. Adelais knew that no natural power could dissuade him; he would go back with her; but she knew how constantly he had hoped for liberty, with what fortitude he had awaited his chance of liberty; and that he should return to captivity, smiling, thrilled her to impotent, heart-shaking rage. It maddened her that he dared love her thus infinitely.

"But, mademoiselle," Fulke d'Arnaye went on, when she had mounted, "let us proceed, if it so please you, by way of Filby. For then we may ride a little distance with this rogue Olivier. I may not hope to see Olivier again in this life, you comprehend, and Olivier is, I think, the one person who loves me in all this great wide world. Me, I am not very popular, you conceive. But you do not object, mademoiselle?"

"No!" she said, in a stifled voice.

Afterward they rode on the way to Filby, leaving Roger Darke to regain at discretion the mastership of his faculties. The two Frenchmen as they went talked vehemently; and Adelais, following them, brooded on the powerful Marquis of Falmouth and the great lady she would shortly be; but her eyes strained after Fulke d'Arnaye.

Presently he fell a-singing; and still his singing praised her in a desirous song, yearning but very sweet, as they rode through the autumn woods; and his voice quickened her pulses as always it had the power to quicken them, and in her soul an interminable battling dragged on.

Sang Fulke d'Arnaye:

> *"Had you lived when earth was new*
> *What had bards of old to do*
> *Save to sing in praise of you?*
>
> *"They had sung of you always,*
> *Adelais, sweet Adelais,*
> *As worthiest of all men's praise;*
> *Nor had undying melodies,*
> *Wailed soft as love may sing of these*
> *Dream-hallowed names,—of Héloïse,*
> *Ysoude, Salomê, Semelê,*
> *Morgaine, Lucrece, Antiopê,*

Brunhilda, Helen, Mélusine,
Penelope, and Magdalene:
—But you alone had all men's praise,
Sweet Adelais"

5. *"Thalatta!"*

WHEN THEY HAD CROSSED THE Bure, they had come into the open country,—a great plain, gray in the moonlight, that descended, hillock by hillock, toward the shores of the North Sea. On the right the dimpling lustre of tumbling waters stretched to a dubious sky-line, unbroken save for the sail of the French boat, moored near the ruins of the old Roman station, Garianonum, and showing white against the unresting sea, like a naked arm; to the left the lights of Filby flashed their unblinking, cordial radiance.

Here the brothers parted. Vainly Olivier wept and stormed before Fulke's unwavering smile; the Sieur d'Arnaye was adamantean: and presently the younger man kissed him on both cheeks and rode slowly away toward the sea.

D'Arnaye stared after him. "Ah, the brave lad!" said Fulke d'Arnaye. "And yet how foolish! Look you, mademoiselle, that rogue is worth ten of me, and he does not even suspect it."

His composure stung her to madness.

"Now, by the passion of our Lord and Saviour!" Adelais cried, wringing her hands in impotence; "I conjure you to hear me, Fulke! You must not do this thing. Oh, you are cruel, cruel! Listen, my lord," she went on with more restraint, when she had reined up her horse by the side of his, "yonder in France the world lies at your feet. Our great King is dead. France rises now, and France needs a brave captain. You, you! it is you that she needs. She has sent for you, my lord, that mother France whom you love. And you will go back to sleep in the sun at Winstead when France has need of you. Oh, it is foul!"

But he shook his head. "France is very dear to me," he said, "yet there are other men who can serve France. And there is no man save me who may tonight serve you, most beautiful lady."

"You shame me!" she cried, in a gust of passion. "You shame my worthlessness with this mad honor of yours that drags you jesting to your death! For you must die a prisoner now, without any hope. You and Orleans and Bourbon are England's only hold on France, and

Bedford dare not let you go. Fetters, chains, dungeons, death, torture perhaps—that is what you must look for now. And you will no longer be held at Winstead, but in the strong Tower at London."

"Hélas, you speak more truly than an oracle," he gayly assented.

And hers was the ageless thought of women. "This man is rather foolish and peculiarly dear to me. What shall I do with him? and how much must I humor him in his foolishness?"

D'Arnaye stayed motionless: but still his eyes strained after Olivier.

Well, she would humor him. There was no alternative save that of perhaps never seeing Fulke again.

Adelais laid her hand upon his arm. "You love me. God knows, I am not worthy of it, but you love me. Ever since I was a child you have loved me,—always, always it was you who indulged me, shielded me, protected me with this fond constancy that I have not merited. Very well,"—she paused, for a single heartbeat,—"go! and take me with you."

The hand he raised shook as though palsied. "O most beautiful!" the Frenchman cried, in an extreme of adoration; "you would do that! You would do that in pity to save me—unworthy me! And it is I whom you call brave—me, who annoy you with my woes so petty!" Fulke d'Arnaye slipped from his horse, and presently stood beside the gray mare, holding a small, slim hand in his. "I thank you," he said, simply. "You know that it is impossible. But yes, I have loved you these long years. And now—Ah, my heart shakes, my words tumble, I cannot speak! You know that I may not—may not let you do this thing. Why, but even if, of your prodigal graciousness, mademoiselle, you were so foolish as to waste a little liking upon my so many demerits—" He gave a hopeless gesture. "Why, there is always our brave marquis to be considered, who will so soon make you a powerful, rich lady. And I?—I have nothing."

But Adelais had rested either hand upon a stalwart shoulder, bending down to him till her hair brushed his. Yes, this man was peculiarly dear to her: she could not bear to have him murdered when in equity he deserved only to have his jaws boxed for his toplofty nonsense about her; and, after all, she did not much mind humoring him in his foolishness.

"Do you not understand?" she whispered. "Ah, my paladin, do you think I speak in pity? I wished to be a great lady,—yes. Yet always, I think, I loved you, Fulke, but until tonight I had believed that love was only the man's folly, the woman's diversion. See, here is Falmouth's ring." She drew it from her finger, and flung it awkwardly, as every woman throws. Through the moonlight it fell glistening. "Yes, I hungered for

Falmouth's power, but you have shown me that which is above any temporal power. Ever I must crave the highest, Fulke—Ah, fair sweet friend, do not deny me!" Adelais cried, piteously. "Take me with you, Fulke! I will ride with you to the wars, my lord, as your page; I will be your wife, your slave, your scullion. I will do anything save leave you. Lord, it is not the maid's part to plead thus!"

Fulke d'Arnaye drew her warm, yielding body toward him and stood in silence. Then he raised his eyes to heaven. "Dear Lord God," he cried, in a great voice, "I entreat of Thee that if through my fault this woman ever know regret or sorrow I be cast into the nethermost pit of Hell for all eternity!" Afterward he kissed her.

And presently Adelais lifted her head, with a mocking little laugh. "Sorrow!" she echoed. "I think there is no sorrow in all the world. Mount, my lord, mount! See where brother Olivier waits for us yonder."

JUNE 5, 1455——AUGUST 4, 1462

"Fortune fuz par clercs jadis nominée, Qui toi, François,
crie et nomme meurtrière."

S o it came about that Adelais went into France with the great-grandson of Tiburce d'Arnaye: and Fulke, they say, made her a very fair husband. But he had not, of course, much time for love-making.

For in France there was sterner work awaiting Fulke d'Arnaye, and he set about it: through seven dreary years he and Rougemont and Dunois managed, somehow, to bolster up the cause of the fat-witted King of Bourges (as the English then called him), who afterward became King Charles VII of France. But in the February of 1429—four days before the Maid of Domremy set forth from her voice-haunted Bois Chenu to bring about a certain coronation in Rheims Church and in Rouen Square a flamy martyrdom—four days before the coming of the good Lorrainer, Fulke d'Arnaye was slain at Rouvray-en-Beausse in that encounter between the French and the English which history has commemorated as the Battle of the Herrings.

Adelais was wooed by, and betrothed to, the powerful old Comte de Vaudremont; but died just before the date set for this second marriage, in October, 1429. She left two sons: Noël, born in 1425, and Raymond, born in 1426; who were reared by their uncle, Olivier d'Arnaye. It was said of them that Noel was the handsomest man of his times, and Raymond the most shrewd; concerning that you will judge hereafter. Both of these d'Arnayes, on reaching manhood, were identified with the Dauphin's party in the unending squabbles between Charles VII and the future Louis XI.

Now you may learn how Noël d'Arnaye came to be immortalized by a legacy of two hundred and twenty blows from an osierwhip—since (as the testator piously affirms), "chastoy est une belle aulmosne."

V

The Episode Called In Necessity's Mortar

1. "Bon Bec de Paris"

THERE WENT ABOUT THE RUE Saint Jacques a notable shaking of heads on the day that Catherine de Vaucelles was betrothed to François de Montcorbier.

"Holy Virgin!" said the Rue Saint Jacques; "the girl is a fool. Why has she not taken Noël d'Arnaye,—Noël the Handsome? I grant you Noël is an ass, but, then, look you, he is of the nobility. He has the Dauphin's favor. Noël will be a great man when our exiled Dauphin comes back from Geneppe to be King of France. Then, too, she might have had Philippe Sermaise. Sermaise is a priest, of course, and one may not marry a priest, but Sermaise has money, and Sermaise is mad for love of her. She might have done worse. But François! Ho, death of my life, what is François? Perhaps—he, he!—perhaps Ysabeau de Montigny might inform us, you say? Doubtless Ysabeau knows more of him than she would care to confess, but I measure the lad by other standards. François is inoffensive enough, I dare assert, but what does Catherine see in him? He is a scholar?—well, the College of Navarre has furnished food for the gallows before this. A poet?—rhyming will not fill the pot. Rhymes are a thin diet for two lusty young folk like these. And who knows if Guillaume de Villon, his foster-father, has one sou to rub against another? He is canon at Saint Benôit-le-Bétourné yonder, but canons are not Midases. The girl will have a hard life of it, neighbor, a hard life, I tell you, if—but, yes!—if Ysabeau de Montigny does not knife her some day. Oh, beyond doubt, Catherine has played the fool."

Thus far the Rue Saint Jacques.

This was on the day of the Fête-Dieu. It was on this day that Noël d'Arnaye blasphemed for a matter of a half-hour and then went to the Crowned Ox, where he drank himself into a contented insensibility; that Ysabeau de Montigny, having wept a little, sent for Gilles Raguyer, a priest and aforetime a rival of François de Montcorbier for her favors; and that Philippe Sermaise grinned and said nothing. But afterward

Sermaise gnawed at his under lip like a madman as he went about seeking for François de Montcorbier.

2. *"Deux estions, et n'avions qu'ung Cueur"*

IT VERGED UPON NINE IN the evening—a late hour in those days—when François climbed the wall of Jehan de Vaucelles' garden.

A wall!—and what is a wall to your true lover? What bones, pray, did the Sieur Pyramus, that ill-starred Babylonish knight, make of a wall? did not his protestations slip through a chink, mocking at implacable granite and more implacable fathers? Most assuredly they did; and Pyramus was a pattern to all lovers. Thus ran the meditations of Master François as he leapt down into the garden.

He had not, you must understand, seen Catherine for three hours. Three hours! three eternities rather, and each one of them spent in Malebolge. Coming to a patch of moonlight, François paused there and cut an agile caper, as he thought of that approaching time when he might see Catherine every day.

"Madame François de Montcorbier," he said, tasting each syllable with gusto. "Catherine de Montcorbier. Was there ever a sweeter juxtaposition of sounds? It is a name for an angel. And an angel shall bear it,—eh, yes, an angel, no less. O saints in Paradise, envy me! Envy me," he cried, with a heroical gesture toward the stars, "for François would change places with none of you."

He crept through ordered rows of chestnuts and acacias to a window wherein burned a dim light. He unslung a lute from his shoulder and began to sing, secure in the knowledge that deaf old Jehan de Vaucelles was not likely to be disturbed by sound of any nature till that time when it should please high God that the last trump be noised about the tumbling heavens.

It was good to breathe the mingled odor of roses and mignonette that was thick about him. It was good to sing to her a wailing song of unrequited love and know that she loved him. François dallied with his bliss, parodied his bliss, and—as he complacently reflected,—lamented in the moonlight with as tuneful a dolor as Messire Orpheus may have evinced when he carolled in Hades.

Sang François:

> *"O Beauty of her, whereby I am undone!*
> *O Grace of her, that hath no grace for me!*

O Love of her, the bit that guides me on
To sorrow and to grievous misery!
O felon Charms, my poor heart's enemy!
O furtive murderous Pride! O pitiless, great
Cold Eyes of her! have done with cruelty!
Have pity upon me ere it be too late!

"Happier for me if elsewhere I had gone
For pity—ah, far happier for me,
Since never of her may any grace be won,
And lest dishonor slay me, I must flee.
'Haro!' I cry, (and cry how uselessly!)
'Haro!' I cry to folk of all estate,

"For I must die unless it chance that she
Have pity upon me ere it be too late.

"M'amye, that day in whose disastrous sun
Your beauty's flower must fade and wane and be
No longer beautiful, draws near,—whereon
I will nor plead nor mock;—not I, for we
Shall both be old and vigorless! M'amye,
Drink deep of love, drink deep, nor hesitate
Until the spring run dry, but speedily
Have pity upon me—ere it be too late!

"Lord Love, that all love's lordship hast in fee,
Lighten, ah, lighten thy displeasure's weight,
For all true hearts should, of Christ's charity,
Have pity upon me ere it be too late."

Then from above a delicate and cool voice was audible. "You have mistaken the window, Monsieur de Montcorbier. Ysabeau de Montigny dwells in the Rue du Fouarre."

"Ah, cruel!" sighed François. "Will you never let that kite hang upon the wall?"

"It is all very well to groan like a bellows. Guillemette Moreau did not sup here for nothing. I know of the verses you made her,—and the gloves you gave her at Candlemas, too. Saint Anne!" observed the voice, somewhat sharply; "she needed gloves. Her hands are so much raw beef. And the head-dress at Easter,—she looks like the steeple of Saint Benoit in it. But every man to his taste, Monsieur de Montcorbier. Good-night, Monsieur de Montcorbier." But, for all that, the window did not close.

"Catherine—!" he pleaded; and under his breath he expressed uncharitable aspirations as to the future of Guillemette Moreau.

"You have made me very unhappy," said the voice, with a little sniff.

"It was before I knew you, Catherine. The stars are beautiful, m'amye, and a man may reasonably admire them; but the stars vanish and are forgotten when the sun appears."

"Ysabeau is not a star," the voice pointed out; "she is simply a lank, good-for-nothing, slovenly trollop."

"Ah, Catherine—!"

"You are still in love with her."

"Catherine—!"

"Otherwise, you will promise me for the future to avoid her as you would the Black Death."

"Catherine, her brother is my friend—!"

"René de Montigny is, to the knowledge of the entire Rue Saint Jacques, a gambler and a drunkard and, in all likelihood, a thief. But you prefer, it appears, the Montignys to me. An ill cat seeks an ill rat. Very heartily do I wish you joy of them. You will not promise? Good-night, then, Monsieur de Montcorbier."

"Mother of God! I promise, Catherine."

From above Mademoiselle de Vaucelles gave a luxurious sigh. "Dear François!" said she.

"You are a tyrant," he complained. "Madame Penthesilea was not more cruel. Madame Herodias was less implacable, I think. And I think that neither was so beautiful."

"I love you," said Mademoiselle de Vaucelles, promptly.

"But there was never any one so many fathoms deep in love as I. Love bandies me from the postern to the frying-pan, from hot to cold. Ah, Catherine, Catherine, have pity upon my folly! Bid me fetch you Prester John's beard, and I will do it; bid me believe the sky is made of calf-skin, that morning is evening, that a fat sow is a windmill, and I will do it. Only love me a little, dear."

"My king, my king of lads!" she murmured.

"My queen, my tyrant of unreason! Ah, yes, you are all that is ruthless and abominable, but then what eyes you have! Oh, very pitiless, large, lovely eyes—huge sapphires that in the old days might have ransomed every monarch in Tamerlane's stable! Even in the night I see them, Catherine."

"Yet Ysabeau's eyes are brown."

"Then are her eyes the gutter's color. But Catherine's eyes are twin firmaments."

And about them the acacias rustled lazily, and the air was sweet with the odors of growing things, and the world, drenched in moonlight, slumbered. Without was Paris, but old Jehan's garden-wall cloistered Paradise.

"Has the world, think you, known lovers, long dead now, that were once as happy as we?"

"Love was not known till we discovered it."

"I am so happy, François, that I fear death."

"We have our day. Let us drink deep of love, not waiting until the spring run dry. Catherine, death comes to all, and yonder in the church-yard the poor dead lie together, huggermugger, and a man may not tell an archbishop from a rag-picker. Yet they have exulted in their youth, and have laughed in the sun with some lass or another lass. We have our day, Catherine."

"Our day wherein I love you!"

"And wherein I love you precisely seven times as much!"

So they prattled in the moonlight. Their discourse was no more overburdened with wisdom than has been the ordinary communing of lovers since Adam first awakened ribless. Yet they were content, who were young in the world's recaptured youth.

Fate grinned and went on with her weaving.

3. "Et Ysabeau, Qui Dit: Enné!"

SOMEWHAT LATER FRANÇOIS CAME DOWN the deserted street, treading on air. It was a bland summer night, windless, moon-washed, odorous with garden-scents; the moon, nearing its full, was a silver egg set on end—("Leda-hatched," he termed it; "one may look for the advent of Queen Heleine ere dawn"); and the sky he likened to blue velvet studded with the gilt nail-heads of a seraphic upholsterer. François was a poet, but a civic poet; then, as always, he pilfered his similes from shop-windows.

But the heart of François was pure magnanimity, the heels of François were mercury, as he tripped past the church of Saint Benoit-le-Bétourné, stark snow and ink in the moonlight. Then with a jerk François paused.

On a stone bench before the church sat Ysabeau de Montigny and Gilles Raguyer. The priest was fuddled, hiccuping in his amorous dithyrambics as he paddled with the girl's hand. "You tempt me to murder," he was saying. "It is a deadly sin, my soul, and I have no mind to fry in Hell while my body swings on the Saint Denis road, a crow's dinner. Let François live, my soul! My soul, he would stick little Gilles like a pig."

Raguyer began to blubber at the thought.

"Holy Macaire!" said François; "here is a pretty plot a-brewing." Yet because his heart was filled just now with loving-kindness, he forgave the girl. *"Tantaene irae?"* said François; and aloud, "Ysabeau, it is time you were abed."

She wheeled upon him in apprehension; then, with recognition, her rage flamed. "Now, Gilles!" cried Ysabeau de Montigny; "now, coward! He is unarmed, Gilles. Look, Gilles! Kill for me this betrayer of women!"

Under his mantle Francois loosened the short sword he carried. But the priest plainly had no mind to the business. He rose, tipsily fumbling a knife, and snarling like a cur at sight of a strange mastiff. "Vile rascal!" said Gilles Raguyer, as he strove to lash himself into a rage. "O coward! O parricide! O Tarquin!"

François began to laugh. "Let us have done with this farce," said he. "Your man has no stomach for battle, Ysabeau. And you do me wrong, my lass, to call me a betrayer of women. Doubtless, that tale seemed the most apt to kindle in poor Gilles some homicidal virtue: but you and I and God know that naught has passed between us save a few kisses and a trinket or so. It is no knifing matter. Yet for the sake of old time, come home, Ysabeau; your brother is my friend, and the hour is somewhat late for honest women to be abroad."

"Enné?" shrilled Ysabeau; "and yet, if I cannot strike a spark of courage from this clod here, there come those who may help me, François de Montcorbier. 'Ware Sermaise, Master François!"

François wheeled. Down the Rue Saint Jacques came Philippe Sermaise, like a questing hound, with drunken Jehan le Merdi at his heels. "Holy Virgin!" thought François; "this is likely to be a nasty affair. I would give a deal for a glimpse of the patrol lanterns just now."

He edged his way toward the cloister, to get a wall at his back. But Gilles Raguyer followed him, knife in hand. "O hideous Tarquin! O Absalom!" growled Gilles; "have you, then, no respect for churchmen?"

With an oath, Sermaise ran up. "Now, may God die twice," he panted, "if I have not found the skulker at last! There is a crow needs picking between us two, Montcorbier."

Hemmed in by his enemies, François temporized. "Why do you accost me thus angrily, Master Philippe?" he babbled. "What harm have I done you? What is your will of me?"

But his fingers tore feverishly at the strap by which the lute was swung over his shoulder, and now the lute fell at their feet, leaving François unhampered and his sword-arm free.

This was fuel to the priest's wrath. "Sacred bones of Benoit!" he snarled; "I could make a near guess as to what window you have been caterwauling under."

From beneath his gown he suddenly hauled out a rapier and struck at the boy while Francois was yet tugging at his sword.

Full in the mouth Sermaise struck him, splitting the lower lip through. Francois felt the piercing cold of the steel, the tingling of it against his teeth, then the warm grateful spurt of blood; through a red mist, he saw Gilles and Ysabeau run screaming down the Rue Saint Jacques.

He drew and made at Sermaise, forgetful of le Merdi. It was shrewd work. Presently they were fighting in the moonlight, hammer-and-tongs, as the saying is, and presently Sermaise was cursing like a madman, for François had wounded him in the groin. Window after window rattled open as the Rue Saint Jacques ran nightcapped to peer at the brawl. Then as Francois hurled back his sword to slash at the priest's shaven head—Frenchmen had not yet learned to thrust with the point in the Italian manner—Jehan le Merdi leapt from behind, nimble as a snake, and wrested away the boy's weapon. Sermaise closed with a glad shout.

"Heart of God!" cried Sermaise. "Pray, bridegroom, pray!"

But François jumped backward, tumbling over le Merdi, and with apish celerity caught up a great stone and flung it full in the priest's countenance.

The rest was hideous. For a breathing space Sermaise kept his feet, his outspread arms making a tottering cross. It was curious to see him peer about irresolutely now that he had no face. François, staring at the black featureless horror before him, began to choke. Standing thus, with outstretched arms, the priest first let fall his hands, so that they hung limp from the wrists; his finger-nails gleamed in the moonlight. His rapier tinkled on the flagstones with the sound of shattering glass, and Philippe Sermaise slid down, all a-jumble, crumpling like a broken toy. Afterward you might have heard a long, awed sibilance go about the windows overhead as the watching Rue Saint Jacques breathed again.

Francois de Montcorbier ran. He tore at his breast as he ran, stifling. He wept as he ran through the moon-washed Rue Saint Jacques, making animal-like and whistling noises. His split lip was a clammy dead thing that napped against his chin as he ran.

"François!" a man cried, meeting him; "ah, name of a name, François!"

It was René de Montigny, lurching from the Crowned Ox, half-tipsy. He caught the boy by the shoulder and hurried François, still sobbing, to Fouquet the barber-surgeon's, where they sewed up his wound. In accordance with the police regulations, they first demanded an account of how he had received it. René lied up-hill and down-dale, while in a corner of the room François monotonously wept.

Fate grinned and went on with her weaving.

4. *"Necessité Faict Gens Mesprende"*

The Rue Saint Jacques had toothsome sauce for its breakfast. The quarter smacked stiff lips over the news, as it pictured François de Montcorbier dangling from Montfaucon. "Horrible!" said the Rue Saint Jacques, and drew a moral of suitably pious flavor.

Guillemette Moreau had told Catherine of the affair before the day was aired. The girl's hurt vanity broke tether.

"Sermaise!" said she. "Bah, what do I care for Sermaise! He killed him in fair fight. But within an hour, Guillemette,—within a half-hour after leaving me, he is junketing on church-porches with that trollop. They were not there for holy-water. Midnight, look you! And he swore to me—chaff, chaff! His honor is chaff, Guillemette, and his heart a bran-bag. Oh, swine, filthy swine! Eh, well, let the swine stick to his sty. Send Noël d'Arnaye to me."

The Sieur d'Arnaye came, his head tied in a napkin.

"Foh!" said she; "another swine fresh from the gutter? No, this is a bottle, a tun, a walking wine-barrel! Noël, I despise you. I will marry you if you like."

He fell to mumbling her hand. An hour later Catherine told Jehan de Vaucelles she intended to marry Noël the Handsome when he should come back from Geneppe with the exiled Dauphin. The old man, having wisdom, lifted his brows, and returned to his reading in *Le Pet au Diable*.

The patrol had transported Sermaise to the prison of Saint Benoit, where he lay all night. That day he was carried to the hospital of the Hôtel Dieu. He died the following Saturday.

Death exalted the man to some nobility. Before one of the apparitors of the Châtelet he exonerated Montcorbier, under oath, and asked that no steps be taken against him. "I forgive him my death," said Sermaise, manly enough at the last, "by reason of certain causes moving him thereunto." Presently he demanded the peach-colored silk glove they would find in the pocket of his gown. It was Catherine's glove. The priest kissed it, and then began to laugh. Shortly afterward he died, still gnawing at the glove.

François and René had vanished. "Good riddance," said the Rue Saint Jacques. But Montcorbier was summoned to answer before the court of the Châtelet for the death of Philippe Sermaise, and in default of his appearance, was subsequently condemned to banishment from the kingdom.

The two young men were at Saint Pourçain-en-Bourbonnais, where René had kinsmen. Under the name of des Loges, François had there secured a place as tutor, but when he heard that Sermaise in the article of death had cleared him of all blame, François set about procuring a pardon.* It was January before he succeeded in obtaining it.

Meanwhile he had learned a deal of René's way of living. "You are a thief," François observed to Montigny the day the pardon came, "but you have played a kindly part by me. I think you are Dysmas, René, not Gestas. Heh, I throw no stones. You have stolen, but I have killed. Let us go to Paris, lad, and start afresh."

Montigny grinned. "I shall certainly go to Paris," he said. "Friends wait for me there,—Guy Tabary, Petit Jehan and Colin de Cayeux. We are planning to visit Guillaume Coiffier, a fat priest with some

---

* There is humor in his deposition that Gilles and Ysabeau and he were loitering before Saint Benoît's in friendly discourse,—"pour soy esbatre." Perhaps René prompted this; but in itself, it is characteristic of Montcorbier that he trenched on perjury, blithely, in order to screen Ysabeau.

six hundred crowns in the cupboard. You will make one of the party, François."

"René, René," said the other, "my heart bleeds for you."

Again Montigny grinned. "You think a great deal about blood nowadays," he commented. "People will be mistaking you for such a poet as was crowned Nero, who, likewise, gave his time to ballad-making and to murdering fathers of the Church. Eh, dear Ahenabarbus, let us first see what the Rue Saint Jacques has to say about your recent gambols. After that, I think you will make one of our party."

5. "Yeulx sans Pitié!"

THERE WAS A LIGHT CRACKLING frost under foot the day that François came back to the Rue Saint Jacques. Upon this brisk, clear January day it was good to be home again, an excellent thing to be alive.

"Eh, Guillemette, Guillemette," he laughed. "Why, lass—!"

"Faugh!" said Guillemette Moreau, as she passed him, nose in air. "A murderer, a priest-killer."

Then the sun went black for François. Such welcoming was a bucket of cold water, full in the face. He gasped, staring after her; and pursy Thomas Tricot, on his way from mass, nudged Martin Blaru in the ribs.

"Martin," said he, "fruit must be cheap this year. Yonder in the gutter is an apple from the gallows-tree, and no one will pick it up."

Blaru turned and spat out, "Cain! Judas!"

This was only a sample. Everywhere François found rigid faces, sniffs, and skirts drawn aside. A little girl in a red cap, Robin Troussecaille's daughter, flung a stone at François as he slunk into the cloister of Saint Benoit-le-Bétourné. In those days a slain priest was God's servant slain, no less; and the Rue Saint Jacques was a respectable God-fearing quarter of Paris.

"My father!" the boy cried, rapping upon the door of the Hôtel de la Porte-Rouge; "O my father, open to me, for I think that my heart is breaking."

Shortly his foster-father, Guillaume de Villon, came to the window. "Murderer!" said he. "Betrayer of women! Now, by the caldron of John! how dare you show your face here? I gave you my name and you soiled it. Back to your husks, rascal!"

"O God, O God!" François cried, one or two times, as he looked up into the old man's implacable countenance. "You, too, my father!"

He burst into a fit of sobbing.

"Go!" the priest stormed; "go, murderer!"

It was not good to hear François' laughter. "What a world we live in!" he giggled. "You gave me your name and I soiled it? Eh, Master Priest, Master Pharisee, beware! *Villon* is good French for *vagabond*, an excellent name for an outcast. And as God lives, I will presently drag that name through every muckheap in France."

Yet he went to Jehan de Vaucelles' home. "I will afford God one more chance at my soul," said François.

In the garden he met Catherine and Noël d'Arnaye coming out of the house. They stopped short. Her face, half-muffled in the brown fur of her cloak, flushed to a wonderful rose of happiness, the great eyes glowed, and Catherine reached out her hands toward François with a glad cry.

His heart was hot wax as he fell before her upon his knees. "O heart's dearest, heart's dearest!" he sobbed; "forgive me that I doubted you!"

And then for an instant, the balance hung level. But after a while, "Ysabeau de Montigny dwells in the Rue du Fouarre," said Catherine, in a crisp voice,—"having served your purpose, however, I perceive that Ysabeau, too, is to be cast aside as though she were an old glove. Monsieur d'Arnaye, thrash for me this betrayer of women."

Noël was a big, handsome man, like an obtuse demi-god, a foot taller than François. Noel lifted the boy by his collar, caught up a stick and set to work. Catherine watched them, her eyes gemlike and cruel.

François did not move a muscle. God had chosen.

After a little, though, the Sieur d'Arnaye flung François upon the ground, where he lay quite still for a moment. Then slowly he rose to his feet. He never looked at Noël. For a long time Francois stared at Catherine de Vaucelles, frost-flushed, defiant, incredibly beautiful. Afterward the boy went out of the garden, staggering like a drunken person.

He found Montigny at the Crowned Ox. "René," said François, "there is no charity on earth, there is no God in Heaven. But in Hell there is most assuredly a devil, and I think that he must laugh a great deal. What was that you were telling me about the priest with six hundred crowns in his cupboard?"

René slapped him on the shoulder. "Now," said he, "you talk like a man." He opened the door at the back and cried: "Colin, you and Petit Jehan and that pig Tabary may come out. I have the honor, messieurs, to offer you a new Companion of the Cockleshell—Master François de Montcorbier."

But the recruit raised a protesting hand. "No," said he,—"François Villon. The name is triply indisputable, since it has been put upon me not by one priest but by three."

6. *"Volia l'Estat Divers d'entre Eulx"*

WHEN THE DAUPHIN CAME FROM Geneppe to be crowned King of France, there rode with him Noël d'Arnaye and Noël's brother Raymond. And the longawaited news that Charles the Well-Served was at last servitor to Death, brought the exiled Louis post-haste to Paris, where the Rue Saint Jacques turned out full force to witness his triumphal entry. They expected, in those days, Saturnian doings of Louis XI, a recrudescence of the Golden Age; and when the new king began his reign by granting Noël a snug fief in Picardy, the Rue Saint Jacques applauded.

"Noël has followed the King's fortunes these ten years," said the Rue Saint Jacques; "it is only just. And now, neighbor, we may look to see Noel the Handsome and Catherine de Vaucelles make a match of it. The girl has a tidy dowry, they say; old Jehan proved wealthier than the quarter suspected. But death of my life, yes! You may see his tomb in the Innocents' yonder, with weeping seraphim and a yard of Latin on it. I warrant you that rascal Montcorbier has lain awake in half the prisons in France thinking of what he flung away. Seven years, no less, since he and Montigny showed their thieves' faces here. La, the world wags, neighbor, and they say there will be a new tax on salt if we go to war with the English."

Not quite thus, perhaps, ran the meditations of Catherine de Vaucelles one still August night as she sat at her window, overlooking the acacias and chestnuts of her garden. Noël, conspicuously prosperous in blue and silver, had but now gone down the Rue Saint Jacques, singing, clinking the fat purse whose plumpness was still a novelty. That evening she had given her promise to marry him at Michaelmas.

This was a black night, moonless, windless. There were a scant half-dozen stars overhead, and the thick scent of roses and mignonette came up to her in languid waves. Below, the tree-tops conferred, stealthily, and the fountain plashed its eternal remonstrance against the conspiracy they lisped of.

After a while Catherine rose and stood contemplative before a long mirror that was in her room. Catherine de Vaucelles was now, at twenty-three, in the full flower of her comeliness. Blue eyes the mirror showed her,—luminous and tranquil eyes, set very far apart; honey-colored hair massed heavily about her face, a mouth all curves, the hue of a strawberry, tender but rather fretful, and beneath it a firm chin; only her nose left something to be desired,—for that feature, though well-formed, was diminutive and bent toward the left, by perhaps the thickness of a cobweb. She might reasonably have smiled at what the mirror showed her, but, for all that, she sighed.

"O Beauty of her, whereby I am undone," said Catherine, wistfully. "Ah, God in Heaven, forgive me for my folly! Sweet Christ, intercede for me who have paid dearly for my folly!"

Fate grinned in her weaving. Through the open window came the sound of a voice singing.

Sang the voice:

> *"O Beauty of her, whereby I am undone!*
> *O Grace of her, that hath no grace for me!*
> *O Love of her, the bit that guides me on*
> *To sorrow and to grievous misery!*
> *O felon Charms, my poor heart's enemy—"*

and the singing broke off in a fit of coughing.

Catherine had remained motionless for a matter of two minutes, her head poised alertly. She went to the gong and struck it seven or eight times.

"Macée, there is a man in the garden. Bring him to me, Macée,—ah, love of God, Macée, make haste!"

Blinking, he stood upon the threshold. Then, without words, their lips met.

"My king!" said Catherine; "heart's emperor!"

"O rose of all the world!" he cried.

There was at first no need of speech.

But after a moment she drew away and stared at him. François, though he was but thirty, seemed an old man. His bald head shone in the candle-light. His face was a mesh of tiny wrinkles, wax-white, and his lower lip, puckered by the scar of his wound, protruded in an eternal grimace. As Catherine steadfastly regarded him, the faded eyes, half-covered with a bluish film, shifted, and with a jerk he glanced over his shoulder. The movement started a cough tearing at his throat.

"Holy Macaire!" said he. "I thought that somebody, if not Henri Cousin, the executioner, was at my heels. Why do you stare so, lass? Have you anything to eat? I am famished."

In silence she brought him meat and wine, and he fell upon it. He ate hastily, chewing with his front teeth, like a sheep.

When he had ended, Catherine came to him and took both his hands in hers and lifted them to her lips. "The years have changed you, François," she said, curiously meek.

François put her away. Then he strode to the mirror and regarded it intently. With a snarl, he turned about. "The years!" said he. "You are modest. It was you who killed François de Montcorbier, as surely as Montcorbier killed Sermaise. Eh, Sovereign Virgin! that is scant cause for grief. You made François Villon. What do you think of him, lass?"

She echoed the name. It was in many ways a seasoned name, but unaccustomed to mean nothing. Accordingly François sneered.

"Now, by all the fourteen joys and sorrows of Our Lady! I believe that you have never heard of François Villon! The Rue Saint Jacques has not heard of François Villon! The pigs, the gross pigs, that dare not peep out of their sty! Why, I have capped verses with the Duke of Orleans. The very street-boys know my Ballad of the Women of Paris. Not a drunkard in the realm but has ranted my jolly Orison for Master Cotard's Soul when the bottle passed. The King himself hauled me out of Meung gaol last September, swearing that in all France there was not my equal at a ballad. And you have never heard of me!"

Once more a fit of coughing choked him mid-course in his indignant chattering.

She gave him a woman's answer: "I do not care if you are the greatest lord in the kingdom or the most sunken knave that steals ducks from Paris Moat. I only know that I love you, François."

For a long time he kept silence, blinking, peering quizzically at her lifted face. She did love him; no questioning that. But presently he again put her aside, and went toward the open window. This was a matter for consideration.

The night was black as a pocket. Staring into it, François threw back his head and drew a deep, tremulous breath. The rising odor of roses and mignonette, keen and intolerably sweet, had roused unforgotten pulses in his blood, had set shame and joy adrum in his breast.

The woman loved him! Through these years, with a woman's unreasoning fidelity, she had loved him. He knew well enough how matters stood between her and Noel d'Arnaye; the host of the Crowned Ox had been garrulous that evening. But it was François whom she loved. She was well-to-do. Here for the asking was a competence, love, an ingleside of his own. The deuce of it was that Francois feared to ask.

"—Because I am still past reason in all that touches this ignorant, hot-headed, Pharisaical, rather stupid wench! That is droll. But love is a resistless tyrant, and, Mother of God! has there been in my life a day, an hour, a moment when I have not loved her! To see her once was all that I had craved,—as a lost soul might covet, ere the Pit take him, one splendid glimpse of Heaven and the Nine Blessed Orders at their fiddling. And I find that she loves me—me! Fate must have her jest, I perceive, though the firmament crack for it. She would have been content enough with Noel, thinking me dead. And with me?" Contemplatively he spat out of the window. "Eh, if I dared hope that this last flicker of life left in my crazy carcass might burn clear! I have but a little while to live; if I dared hope to live that little cleanly! But the next cup of wine, the next light woman?—I have answered more difficult riddles. Choose, then, François Villon,—choose between the squalid, foul life yonder and her well-being. It is true that starvation is unpleasant and that hanging is reported to be even less agreeable. But just now these considerations are irrelevant."

Staring into the darkness he fought the battle out. Squarely he faced the issue; for that instant he saw François Villon as the last seven years had made him, saw the wine-sodden soul of François Villon, rotten and weak and honeycombed with vice. Moments of nobility it had; momentarily, as now, it might be roused to finer issues; but François knew that no power existent could hearten it daily to curb the brutish passions. It was no longer possible for François Villon to live cleanly. "For what am I?—a hog with a voice. And shall I hazard her life's happiness to get me a more comfortable sty? Ah, but the deuce of it is that I so badly need that sty!"

He turned with a quick gesture.

"Listen," François said. "Yonder is Paris,—laughing, tragic Paris, who once had need of a singer to proclaim her splendor and all her misery. Fate made the man; in necessity's mortar she pounded his soul into the shape Fate needed. To king's courts she lifted him; to thieves' hovels she thrust him down; and past Lutetia's palaces and abbeys and taverns and lupanars and gutters and prisons and its very gallows—past each in turn the man was dragged, that he might make the Song of Paris. He could not have made it here in the smug Rue Saint Jacques. Well! the song is made, Catherine. So long as Paris endures, François Villon will be remembered. Villon the singer Fate fashioned as was needful: and, in this fashioning, Villon the man was damned in body and soul. And by God! the song was worth it!"

She gave a startled cry and came to him, her hands fluttering toward his breast. "François!" she breathed.

It would not be good to kill the love in her face.

"You loved François de Montcorbier. François de Montcorbier is dead. The Pharisees of the Rue Saint Jacques killed him seven years ago, and that day François Villon was born. That was the name I swore to drag through every muckheap in France. And I have done it, Catherine. The Companions of the Cockleshell—eh, well, the world knows us. We robbed Guillamme Coiffier, we robbed the College of Navarre, we robbed the Church of Saint Maturin,—I abridge the list of our gambols. Now we harvest. René de Montigny's bones swing in the wind yonder at Montfaucon. Colin de Cayeux they broke on the wheel. The rest—in effect, I am the only one that justice spared,—because I had diverting gifts at rhyming, they said. Pah! if they only knew! I am immortal, lass. *Exegi monumentum*. Villon's glory and Villon's shame will never die."

He flung back his bald head and laughed now, tittering over that calamitous, shabby secret between all-seeing God and François Villon. She had drawn a little away from him. This well-reared girl saw him exultant in infamy, steeped to the eyes in infamy. But still the nearness of her, the faint perfume of her, shook in his veins, and still he must play the miserable comedy to the end, since the prize he played for was to him peculiarly desirable.

"A thief—a common thief!" But again her hands fluttered back. "I drove you to it. Mine is the shame."

"Holy Macaire! what is a theft or two? Hunger that causes the wolf to sally from the wood, may well make a man do worse than steal. I could tell you—For example, you might ask in Hell of one Thevenin Pensete, who knifed him in the cemetery of Saint John."

He hinted a lie, for it was Montigny who killed Thevenin Pensete. Villon played without scruple now.

Catherine's face was white. "Stop," she pleaded; "no more, François,—ah, Holy Virgin! do not tell me any more."

But after a little she came to him, touching him almost as if with unwillingness. "Mine is the shame. It was my jealousy, my vanity, François, that thrust you back into temptation. And we are told by those in holy orders that the compassion of God is infinite. If you still care for me, I will be your wife."

Yet she shuddered.

He saw it. His face, too, was paper, and François laughed horribly.

"If I still love you! Go, ask of Denise, of Jacqueline, or of Pierrette, of Marion the Statue, of Jehanne of Brittany, of Blanche Slippermaker, of Fat Peg,—ask of any trollop in all Paris how François Villon loves. You thought me faithful! You thought that I especially preferred you to any other bed-fellow! Eh, I perceive that the credo of the Rue Saint Jacques is somewhat narrow-minded. For my part I find one woman much the same as another." And his voice shook, for he saw how pretty she was, saw how she suffered. But he managed a laugh.

"I do not believe you," Catherine said, in muffled tones. "François! You loved me, François. Ah, boy, boy!" she cried, with a pitiable wail; "come back to me, boy that I loved!"

It was a difficult business. But he grinned in her face.

"He is dead. Let François de Montcorbier rest in his grave. Your voice is very sweet, Catherine, and—and he could refuse you nothing, could he, lass? Ah, God, God, God!" he cried, in his agony; "why can you not believe me? I tell you Necessity pounds us in her mortar to what shape she will. I tell you that Montcorbier loved you, but François Villon prefers Fat Peg. An ill cat seeks an ill rat." And with this, tranquillity fell upon his soul, for he knew that he had won.

Her face told him that. Loathing was what he saw there.

"I am sorry," Catherine said, dully. "I am sorry. Oh, for high God's sake! go, go! Do you want money? I will give you anything if you will only go. Oh, beast! Oh, swine, swine, swine!"

He turned and went, staggering like a drunken person.

Once in the garden he fell prone upon his face in the wet grass. About him the mingled odor of roses and mignonette was sweet and heavy; the fountain plashed interminably in the night, and above him the chestnuts and acacias rustled and lisped as they had done seven years ago. Only he was changed.

"O Mother of God," the thief prayed, "grant that Noël may be kind to her! Mother of God, grant that she may be happy! Mother of God, grant that I may not live long!"

And straightway he perceived that triple invocation could be, rather neatly, worked out in ballade form. Yes, with a separate prayer to each verse. So, dismissing for the while his misery, he fell to considering, with undried cheeks, what rhymes he needed.

JULY 17, 1484

"Et puis il se rencontre icy une avanture merveilleuse, c'est que le fils de Grand Turc ressemble à Cléonte, à peu de chose prés."

*N*oël d'Arnaye and Catherine de Vaucelles were married in the September of 1462, and afterward withdrew to Noël's fief in Picardy. There Noël built him a new Chateau d'Arnaye, and through the influence of Nicole Beaupertuys, the King's mistress, (who was rumored in court by-ways to have a tenderness for the handsome Noël), obtained large grants for its maintenance. Madame d'Arnaye, also, it is gratifying to record, appears to have lived in tolerable amity with Sieur Noël, and neither of them pried too closely into the other's friendships.

Catherine died in 1470, and Noël outlived her but by three years. Of the six acknowledged children surviving him, only one was legitimate—a daughter called Matthiette. The estate and title thus reverted to Raymond d'Arnaye, Noël's younger brother, from whom the present family of Arnaye is descended.

Raymond was a far shrewder man than his predecessor. For ten years' space, while Louis XI, that royal fox of France, was destroying feudalism piecemeal,—trimming its power day by day as you might pare an onion,—the new Sieur d'Arnaye steered his shifty course between France and Burgundy, always to the betterment of his chances in this world however he may have modified them in the next. At Arras he fought beneath the oriflamme; at Guinegate you could not have found a more staunch Burgundian: though he was no warrior, victory followed him like a lap-dog. So that presently the Sieur d'Arnaye and the Vicomte de Puysange—with which family we have previously concerned ourselves—were the great lords of Northern France.

But after the old King's death came gusty times for Sieur Raymond. It is with them we have here to do.

VI

THE EPISODE CALLED
THE CONSPIRACY OF ARNAYE

1. *Policy Tempered with Singing*

"AND SO," SAID THE SIEUR d'Arnaye, as he laid down the letter, "we may look for the coming of Monsieur de Puysange tomorrow."

The Demoiselle Matthiette contorted her features in an expression of disapproval. "So soon!" said she. "I had thought—"

"Ouais, my dear niece, Love rides by ordinary with a dripping spur, and is still as arbitrary as in the day when Mars was taken with a net and amorous Jove bellowed in Europa's kail-yard. My faith! if Love distemper thus the spectral ichor of the gods, is it remarkable that the warmer blood of man pulses rather vehemently at his bidding? It were the least of Cupid's miracles that a lusty bridegroom of some twenty-and-odd should be pricked to outstrip the dial by a scant week. For love—I might tell you such tales—"

Sieur Raymond crossed his white, dimpled hands over a well-rounded paunch and chuckled reminiscently; had he spoken doubtless he would have left Master Jehan de Troyes very little to reveal in his Scandalous Chronicle: but now, as if now recalling with whom Sieur Raymond conversed, d'Arnaye's lean face assumed an expression of placid sanctity, and the somewhat unholy flame died out of his green eyes. He was like no other thing than a plethoric cat purring over the follies of kittenhood. You would have taken oath that a cultured taste for good living was the chief of his offences, and that this benevolent gentleman had some sixty well-spent years to his credit. True, his late Majesty, King Louis XI, had sworn Pacque Dieu! that d'Arnaye loved underhanded work so heartily that he conspired with his gardener concerning the planting of cabbages, and within a week after his death would be heading some treachery against Lucifer; but kings are not always infallible, as his Majesty himself had proven at Peronne.

"—For," said the Sieur d'Arnaye, "man's flesh is frail, and the devil is very cunning to avail himself of the weaknesses of lovers."

"Love!" Matthiette cried. "Ah, do not mock me, my uncle! There can be no pretence of love between Monsieur de Puysange and me. A man that I have never seen, that is to wed me of pure policy, may look for no Alcestis in his wife."

"You speak like a very sensible girl," said Sieur Raymond, complacently. "However, so that he find her no Guinevere or Semiramis or other loose-minded trollop of history, I dare say Monsieur de Puysange will hold to his bargain with indifferent content. Look you, niece, he, also, is buying—though the saying is somewhat rustic—a pig in a poke."

Matthiette glanced quickly toward the mirror which hung in her apartment. The glass reflected features which went to make up a beauty already be-sonneted in that part of France; and if her green gown was some months behind the last Italian fashion, it undeniably clad one who needed few adventitious aids. The Demoiselle Matthiette at seventeen was very tall, and was as yet too slender for perfection of form, but her honey-colored hair hung heavily about the unblemished oval of a countenance whose nose alone left something to be desired; for this feature, though well shaped, was unduly diminutive. For the rest, her mouth curved in an irreproachable bow, her complexion was mingled milk and roses, her blue eyes brooded in a provoking calm; taking matters by and large, the smile that followed her inspection of the mirror's depths was far from unwarranted. Catherine de Vaucelles reanimate, you would have sworn; and at the abbey of Saint Maixent-en-Poitou there was a pot-belly monk, a Brother François, who would have demonstrated it to you, in an unanswerable ballad, that Catherine's daughter was in consequence all that an empress should be and so rarely is. Harembourges and Bertha Broadfoot and white Queen Blanche would have been laughed to scorn, demolished and proven, in comparison (with a catalogue of very intimate personal detail), the squalidest sluts conceivable, by Brother François.

But Sieur Raymond merely chuckled wheezily, as one discovering a fault in his companion of which he disapproves in theory, but in practice finds flattering to his vanity.

"I grant you, Monsieur de Puysange drives a good bargain," said Sieur Raymond. "Were Cleopatra thus featured, the Roman lost the world very worthily. Yet, such is the fantastic disposition of man that I do not doubt the vicomte looks forward to the joys of tomorrow no whit more cheerfully than you do: for the lad is young, and, as rumor says, has been guilty of divers verses,—ay, he has bearded common-sense in the vext periods of many a wailing rhyme. I will wager a moderate amount, however, that the vicomte, like a sensible young man, keeps these whimsies of flames and dames laid away in lavender for festivals and the like; they are somewhat too fine for everyday wear."

Sieur Raymond sipped the sugared wine which stood beside him. "Like any sensible young man," he repeated, in a meditative fashion that was half a query.

Matthiette stirred uneasily. "Is love, then, nothing?" she murmured.

"Love!" Sieur Raymond barked like a kicked mastiff. "It is very discreetly fabled that love was brought forth at Cythera by the ocean fogs. Thus, look you, even ballad-mongers admit it comes of a short-lived family, that fade as time wears on. I may have a passion for cloud-tatters, and, doubtless, the morning mists are beautiful; but if I give rein to my admiration, breakfast is likely to grow cold. I deduce that beauty, as represented by the sunrise, is less profitably considered than utility, as personified by the frying-pan. And love! A niece of mine prating of love!" The idea of such an occurrence, combined with a fit of coughing which now came upon him, drew tears to the Sieur d'Arnaye's eyes. "Pardon me," said he, when he had recovered his breath, "if I speak somewhat brutally to maiden ears."

Matthiette sighed. "Indeed," said she, "you have spoken very brutally!" She rose from her seat, and went to the Sieur d'Arnaye. "Dear uncle," said she, with her arms about his neck, and with her soft cheek brushing his withered countenance, "are you come to my apartments tonight to tell me that love is nothing—you who have shown me that even the roughest, most grizzled bear in all the world has a heart compact of love and tender as a woman's?"

The Sieur d'Arnaye snorted. "Her mother all over again!" he complained; and then, recovering himself, shook his head with a hint of sadness.

He said: "I have sighed to every eyebrow at court, and I tell you this moonshine is—moonshine pure and simple. Matthiette, I love you too dearly to deceive you in, at all events, this matter, and I have learned by hard knocks that we of gentle quality may not lightly follow our own inclinations. Happiness is a luxury which the great can very rarely afford. Granted that you have an aversion to this marriage. Yet consider this: Arnaye and Puysange united may sit snug and let the world wag; otherwise, lying here between the Breton and the Austrian, we are so many nuts in a door-crack, at the next wind's mercy. And yonder in the South, Orléans and Dunois are raising every devil in Hell's register! Ah, no, ma mie; I put it to you fairly is it of greater import that a girl have her callow heart's desire than that a province go free of Monsieur War and Madame Rapine?"

"Yes, but—" said Matthiette.

Sieur Raymond struck his hand upon the table with considerable heat. "Everywhere Death yawps at the frontier; will you, a d'Arnaye, bid him enter and surfeit? An alliance with Puysange alone may save us. Eheu, it is, doubtless, pitiful that a maid may not wait and wed her chosen paladin, but our vassals demand these sacrifices. For example, do you think I wedded my late wife in any fervor of adoration? I had never seen her before our marriage day; yet we lived much as most couples do for some ten years afterward, thereby demonstrating—"

He smiled, evilly; Matthiette sighed.

"—Well, thereby demonstrating nothing new," said Sieur Raymond. "So do you remember that Pierre must have his bread and cheese; that the cows must calve undisturbed; that the pigs—you have not seen the sow I had today from Harfleur?—black as ebony and a snout like a rose-leaf!—must be stied in comfort: and that these things may not be, without an alliance with Puysange. Besides, dear niece, it is something to be the wife of a great lord."

A certain excitement awoke in Matthiette's eyes. "It must be very beautiful at Court," said she, softly. "Masques, fêtes, tourneys every day;—and they say the new King is exceedingly gallant—"

Sieur Raymond caught her by the chin, and for a moment turned her face toward his. "I warn you," said he, "you are a d'Arnaye; and King or not—"

He paused here. Through the open window came the voice of one singing to the demure accompaniment of a lute.

"Hey?" said the Sieur d'Arnaye.

Sang the voice:

> "When you are very old, and I am gone,
> Not to return, it may be you will say—
> Hearing my name and holding me as one
> Long dead to you,—in some half-jesting way
> Of speech, sweet as vague heraldings of May

JAMES BRANCH CABELL

> *Rumored in woods when first the throstles sing—*
> *'He loved me once.' And straightway murmuring*
> *My half-forgotten rhymes, you will regret*
> *Evanished times when I was wont to sing*
> *So very lightly, 'Love runs into debt.'"*

"Now, may I never sit among the saints," said the Sieur d'Arnaye, "if that is not the voice of Raoul de Prison, my new page."

"Hush," Matthiette whispered. "He woos my maid, Alys. He often sings under the window, and I wink at it."

Sang the voice:

> *"I shall not heed you then. My course being run*
> *For good or ill, I shall have gone my way,*
> *And know you, love, no longer,—nor the sun,*
> *Perchance, nor any light of earthly day,*
> *Nor any joy nor sorrow,—while at play*
> *The world speeds merrily, nor reckoning*
> *Our coming or our going. Lips will cling,*
> *Forswear, and be forsaken, and men forget*
> *Where once our tombs were, and our children sing—*
> *So very lightly!—'Love runs into debt.'*

> *"If in the grave love have dominion*
> *Will that wild cry not quicken the wise clay,*
> *And taunt with memories of fond deeds undone,—*
> *Some joy untasted, some lost holiday,—*
> *All death's large wisdom? Will that wisdom lay*
> *The ghost of any sweet familiar thing*
> *Come haggard from the Past, or ever bring*
> *Forgetfulness of those two lovers met*
> *When all was April?—nor too wise to sing*
> *So very lightly, 'Love runs into debt.'*

> *"Yet, Matthiette, though vain remembering*
> *Draw nigh, and age be drear, yet in the spring*
> *We meet and kiss, whatever hour beset*
> *Wherein all hours attain to harvesting,—*
> *So very lightly love runs into debt."*

"Dear, dear!" said the Sieur d'Arnaye. "You mentioned your maid's name, I think?"

"Alys," said Matthiette, with unwonted humbleness.

Sieur Raymond spread out his hands in a gesture of commiseration. "This is very remarkable," he said. "Beyond doubt, the gallant beneath has made some unfortunate error. Captain Gotiard," he called, loudly, "will you ascertain who it is that warbles in the garden such queer aliases for our good Alys?"

2. *Age Glosses the Text of Youth*

Gotiard was not long in returning; he was followed by two men-at-arms, who held between them the discomfited minstrel. Envy alone could have described the lutanist as ill-favored; his close-fitting garb, wherein the brave reds of autumn were judiciously mingled, at once set off a well-knit form and enhanced the dark comeliness of features less French than Italian in cast. The young man now stood silent, his eyes mutely questioning the Sieur d'Arnaye.

"Oh, la, la, la!" chirped Sieur Raymond. "Captain, I think you are at liberty to retire." He sipped his wine meditatively, as the men filed out. "Monsieur de Frison," d'Arnaye resumed, when the arras had fallen, "believe me, I grieve to interrupt your very moving and most excellently phrased ballad in this fashion. But the hour is somewhat late for melody, and the curiosity of old age is privileged. May one inquire, therefore, why you outsing my larks and linnets and other musical poultry that are now all abed? and warble them to rest with this pleasing but—if I may venture a suggestion—rather ill-timed madrigal?"

The young man hesitated for an instant before replying. "Sir," said he, at length, "I confess that had I known of your whereabouts, the birds had gone without their lullaby. But you so rarely come to this wing of the chateau, that your presence here tonight is naturally unforeseen. As it is, since chance has betrayed my secret to you, I must make bold to acknowledge it; and to confess that I love your niece."

"Hey, no doubt you do," Sieur Raymond assented, pleasantly. "Indeed, I think half the young men hereabout are in much the same predicament. But, my question, if I mistake not, related to your reason for chaunting canzonets beneath her window."

Raoul de Frison stared at him in amazement. "I love her," he said.

"You mentioned that before," Sieur Raymond suggested. "And I agreed, as I remember, that it was more than probable; for my niece here—though it be I that speak it—is by no means uncomely, has a commendable voice, the walk of a Hebe, and sufficient wit to deceive her lover into happiness. My faith, young man, you show excellent taste! But, I submit, the purest affection is an insufficient excuse for outbaying a whole kennel of hounds beneath the adored one's casement."

"Sir," said Raoul, "I believe that lovers have rarely been remarkable for sanity; and it is an immemorial custom among them to praise the object of their desires with fitting rhymes. Conceive, sir, that in your youth, had you been accorded the love of so fair a lady, you yourself had scarcely done otherwise. For I doubt if your blood runs so thin as yet that you have quite forgot young Raymond d'Arnaye and the gracious ladies whom he loved,—I think that your heart must needs yet treasure the memories of divers moonlit nights, even such as this, when there was a great silence in the world, and the nested trees were astir with desire of the dawn, and your waking dreams were vext with the singular favor of some woman's face. It is in the name of that young Raymond I now appeal to you."

"H'm!" said the Sieur d'Arnaye. "As I understand it, you appeal on the ground that you were coerced by the moonlight and led astray by the bird-nests in my poplar-trees; and you desire me to punish your accomplices rather than you."

"Sir,—" said Raoul.

Sieur Raymond snarled. "You young dog, you know that in the most prosaic breast a minor poet survives his entombment,—and you endeavor to make capital of the knowledge. You know that I have a most sincere affection for your father, and have even contracted since you came to Arnaye more or less tolerance for you,—which emboldens you, my friend, to keep me out of a comfortable bed at this hour of the night with an idiotic discourse of moonlight and dissatisfied shrubbery! As it happens, I am not a lank wench in her first country dance. Remember that, Raoul de Frison, and praise the good God who gave me at birth a very placable disposition! There is not a seigneur in all France, save me, but would hang you at the crack of that same dawn for which you report your lackadaisical trees to be whining; but the quarrel will soon be Monsieur de Puysange's, and I prefer that he settle it at his own discretion. I content myself with advising you to pester my niece no more."

Raoul spoke boldly. "She loves me," said he, standing very erect.

Sieur Raymond glanced at Matthiette, who sat with downcast head. "H'm!" said he. "She moderates her transports indifferently well. Though, again, why not? You are not an ill-looking lad. Indeed, Monsieur de Frison, I am quite ready to admit that my niece is breaking her heart for you. The point on which I wish to dwell is that she weds Monsieur de Puysange early tomorrow morning."

"Uncle," Matthiette cried, as she started to her feet, "such a marriage is a crime! I love Raoul!"

"Undoubtedly," purred Sieur Raymond, "you love the lad unboundedly, madly, distractedly! Now we come to the root of the matter." He sank back in his chair and smiled. "Young people," said he, "be seated, and hearken to the words of wisdom. Love is a divine insanity, in which the sufferer fancies the world mad. And the world is made up of madmen who condemn and punish one another."

"But," Matthiette dissented, "ours is no ordinary case!"

"Surely not," Sieur Raymond readily agreed; "for there was never an ordinary case in all the history of the universe. Oh, but I, too, have known this madness; I, too, have perceived how infinitely my own skirmishes with the blind bow-god differed in every respect from all that has been or will ever be. It is an infallible sign of this frenzy. Surely, I have said, the world will not willingly forget the vision of Chloris in her wedding garments, or the wonder of her last clinging kiss. Or, say Phyllis comes tomorrow: will an uninventive sun dare to rise in the old, hackneyed fashion on such a day of days? Perish the thought! There will probably be six suns, and, I dare say, a meteor or two."

"I perceive, sir," Raoul said here, "that after all you have not forgotten the young Raymond of whom I spoke."

"That was a long while ago," snapped Sieur Raymond. "I know a deal more of the world nowadays; and a level-headed world would be somewhat surprised at such occurrences, and suggest that for the future Phyllis remain at home. For whether you—or I—or any one—be in love or no is to our fellow creatures an affair of astonishingly trivial import. Not since Noé that great admiral, repeopled the world by begetting three sons upon Dame Noria has there been a love-business worthy of consideration; nor, if you come to that, not since sagacious Solomon went a-wenching has a wise man wasted his wisdom on a lover. So love one another, my children, by all means: but do you, Matthiette, make ready to depart into Normandy as a true and faithful wife to Monsieur de Puysange; and do you, Raoul de Prison, remain at Arnaye, and attend to my falcons more carefully than you have done of late,—or, by the cross of Saint Lo! I will clap the wench in a convent and hang the lad as high as Haman!"

Whereon Sieur Raymond smiled pleasantly, and drained his wine-cup as one considering the discussion ended.

Raoul sat silent for a moment. Then he rose. "Monsieur d'Arnaye, you know me to be a gentleman of unblemished descent, and as such entitled to a hearing. I forbid you before all-seeing Heaven to wed your niece to a man she does not love! And I have the honor to request of you her hand in marriage."

"Which offer I decline," said Sieur Raymond, grinning placidly,—"with every imaginable civility. Niece," he continued, "here is a gentleman who offers you a heartful of love, six months of insanity, and forty years of boredom in a leaky, wind-swept château. He has dreamed dreams concerning you: allow me to present to you the reality."

With some ceremony Sieur Raymond now grasped Matthiette's hand and led her mirror-ward. "Permit me to present the wife of Monsieur de Puysange. Could he have made a worthier choice? Ah, happy lord, that shall so soon embrace such perfect loveliness! For, frankly, my niece, is not that golden hair of a shade that will set off a coronet extraordinarily well? Are those wondrous eyes not fashioned to surfeit themselves upon the homage and respect accorded the wife of a great lord? Ouais, the thing is indisputable: and, therefore, I must differ from Monsieur de Frison here, who would condemn this perfection to bloom and bud unnoticed in a paltry country town."

There was an interval, during which Matthiette gazed sadly into the mirror. "And Arnaye—?" said she.

"Undoubtedly," said Sieur Raymond,—"Arnaye must perish unless Puysange prove her friend. Therefore, my niece conquers her natural aversion to a young and wealthy husband, and a life of comfort and flattery and gayety; relinquishes you, Raoul; and, like a feminine Mettius Curtius, sacrifices herself to her country's welfare. Pierre may sleep undisturbed; and the pigs will have a new sty. My faith, it is quite affecting! And so," Sieur Raymond summed it up, "you two young fools may bid adieu, once for all, while I contemplate this tapestry." He strolled to the end of the room and turned his back. "Admirable!" said he; "really now, that leopard is astonishingly lifelike!"

Raoul came toward Matthiette. "Dear love," said he, "you have chosen wisely, and I bow to your decision. Farewell, Matthiette,—O indomitable heart! O brave perfect woman that I have loved! Now at the last of all, I praise you for your charity to me, Love's mendicant,—ah, believe me, Matthiette, that atones for aught which follows now. Come what may, I shall always remember that once in old days you loved me, and, remembering this, I shall always thank God with a contented heart." He bowed over her unresponsive hand. "Matthiette," he whispered, "be happy! For I desire that very heartily, and I beseech of our Sovereign Lady—not caring to hide at all how my voice shakes, nor how the loveliness of you, seen now for the last time, is making blind my eyes—that you may never know unhappiness. You have chosen wisely, Matthiette; yet, ah, my dear, do not forget me utterly, but keep always a little place in your heart for your boy lover!"

Sieur Raymond concluded his inspection of the tapestry, and turned with a premonitory cough. "Thus ends the comedy," said he, shrugging, "with much fine, harmless talking about 'always,' while the world triumphs. Invariably the world triumphs, my children. Eheu, we are as God made us, we men and women that cumber His stately earth!" He drew his arm through Raoul's. "Farewell, niece," said Sieur Raymond, smiling; "I rejoice that you are cured of your malady. Now in respect to gerfalcons—" said he. The arras fell behind them.

3. *Obdurate Love*

MATTHIETTE SAT BROODING IN HER room, as the night wore on. She was pitifully frightened, numb. There was in the room, she dimly noted, a heavy silence that sobs had no power to shatter. Dimly, too, she seemed aware of a multitude of wide, incurious eyes which watched her from every corner, where panels snapped at times with sharp echoes. The night was well-nigh done when she arose.

"After all," she said, wearily, "it is my manifest duty." Matthiette crept to the mirror and studied it.

"Madame de Puysange," said she, without any intonation; then threw her arms above her head, with a hard gesture of despair. "I love him!" she cried, in a frightened voice.

Matthiette went to a great chest and fumbled among its contents. She drew out a dagger in a leather case, and unsheathed it. The light shone evilly scintillant upon the blade. She laughed, and hid it in the bosom of her gown, and fastened a cloak about her with impatient fingers. Then Matthiette crept down the winding stair that led to the gardens, and unlocked the door at the foot of it.

A sudden rush of night swept toward her, big with the secrecy of dawn. The sky, washed clean of stars, sprawled above,—a leaden, monotonous blank. Many trees whispered thickly over the chaos of earth; to the left, in an increasing dove-colored luminousness, a field of growing maize bristled like the chin of an unshaven Titan.

Matthiette entered an expectant world. Once in the tree-chequered gardens, it was as though she crept through the aisles of an unlit cathedral already garnished for its sacred pageant. Matthiette heard the querulous birds call sleepily above; the margin of night was thick with their petulant complaints; behind her was the monstrous shadow of the Chateau d'Arnaye, and past that was a sullen red, the red of contused flesh, to herald dawn. Infinity waited a-tiptoe, tense for the coming miracle, and against this vast repression, her grief dwindled into irrelevancy: the leaves whispered comfort; each tree-bole hid chuckling fauns. Matthiette laughed. Content had flooded the universe all through and through now that yonder, unseen as yet, the scarlet-faced sun was toiling up the rim of the world, and matters, it somehow seemed, could not turn out so very ill, in the end.

Matthiette came to a hut, from whose open window a faded golden glow spread out into obscurity like a tawdry fan. From without she peered into the hut and saw Raoul. A lamp flickered upon the table. His shadow twitched and wavered about the plastered walls,—a portentous mass of head upon a hemisphere of shoulders,—as Raoul bent over a chest, sorting the contents, singing softly to himself, while Matthiette leaned upon the sill without, and the gardens of Arnaye took form and stirred in the heart of a chill, steady, sapphire-like radiance.

Sang Raoul:

> *"Lord, I have worshipped thee ever,—*
> *Through all these years*
> *I have served thee, forsaking never*
> *Light Love that veers*
> *As a child between laughter and tears.*
> *Hast thou no more to afford,—*
> *Naught save laughter and tears,—*
> *Love, my lord?*

"I have borne thy heaviest burden,
Nor served thee amiss:
Now thou hast given a guerdon;
Lo, it was this—
A sigh, a shudder, a kiss.
Hast thou no more to accord!
I would have more than this,
Love, my lord.

"I am wearied of love that is pastime
And gifts that it brings;
I entreat of thee, lord, at this last time

"Inèffable things.
Nay, have proud long-dead kings
Stricken no subtler chord,
Whereof the memory clings,
Love, my lord?

"But for a little we live;
Show me thine innermost hoard!
Hast thou no more to give,
Love, my lord?"

4. *Raymond Psychopompos*

MATTHIETTE WENT TO THE HUT'S door: her hands fell irresolutely upon the rough surface of it and lay still for a moment. Then with the noise of a hoarse groan the door swung inward, and the light guttered in a swirl of keen morning air, casting convulsive shadows upon her lifted countenance, and was extinguished. She held out her arms in a gesture that was half maternal. "Raoul!" she murmured.

He turned. A sudden bird plunged through the twilight without, with a glad cry that pierced like a knife through the stillness which had fallen in the little room. Raoul de Frison faced her, with clenched hands, silent. For that instant she saw him transfigured.

But his silence frightened her. There came a piteous catch in her voice. "Fair friend, have you not bidden me—*be happy?*"

He sighed. "Mademoiselle," he said, dully, "I may not avail myself of your tenderness of heart; that you have come to comfort me in my sorrow is a deed at which, I think, God's holy Angels must rejoice: but I cannot avail myself of it."

"Raoul, Raoul," she said, "do you think that I have come in—pity!"

"Matthiette," he returned, "your uncle spoke the truth. I have dreamed dreams concerning you,—dreams of a foolish, golden-hearted girl, who would yield—yield gladly—all that the world may give, to be one flesh and soul with me. But I have wakened, dear, to the braver reality,—that valorous woman, strong enough to conquer even her own heart that her people may be freed from their peril."

"Blind! blind!" she cried.

Raoul smiled down upon her. "Mademoiselle," said he, "I do not doubt that you love me."

She went wearily toward the window. "I am not very wise," Matthiette said, looking out upon the gardens, "and it appears that God has given me an exceedingly tangled matter to unravel. Yet if I decide it wrongly I think the Eternal Father will understand it is because I am not very wise."

Matthiette for a moment was silent. Then with averted face she spoke again. "My uncle commands me, with many astute saws and pithy sayings, to wed Monsieur de Puysange. I have not skill to combat him. Many times he has proven it my duty, but he is quick in argument and proves what he will; and I do not think it is my duty. It appears to me a matter wherein man's wisdom is at variance with God's will as manifested to us through the holy Evangelists. Assuredly, if I do not wed Monsieur de Puysange there may be war here in our Arnaye, and God has forbidden war; but I may not insure peace in Arnaye without prostituting my body to a man I do not love, and that, too, God has forbidden. I speak somewhat grossly for a maid, but you love me, I think, and will understand. And I, also, love you, Monsieur de Frison. Yet—ah, I am pitiably weak! Love tugs at my heart-strings, bidding me cling to you, and forget these other matters; but I cannot do that, either. I desire very heartily the comfort and splendor and adulation which you cannot give me. I am pitiably weak, Raoul! I cannot come to you with an undivided heart,—but my heart, such as it is, I have given you, and today I deliver my honor into your hands and my life's happiness, to preserve or to destroy. Mother of Christ, grant that I have chosen rightly, for I have chosen now, past retreat! I have chosen you, Raoul, and that love which you elect to give me, and of which I must endeavor to be worthy."

Matthiette turned from the window. Now, her bright audacity gone, her ardors chilled, you saw how like a grave, straightforward boy she was, how illimitably tender, how inefficient. "It may be that I have decided wrongly in this tangled matter," she said now. "And yet I think that God, Who loves us infinitely, cannot be greatly vexed at anything His children do for love of one another."

He came toward her. "I bid you go," he said. "Matthiette, it is my duty to bid you go, and it is your duty to obey."

She smiled wistfully through unshed tears. "Man's wisdom!" said Matthiette. "I think that it is not my duty. And so I disobey you, dear,— this once, and no more hereafter."

"And yet last night—" Raoul began.

"Last night," said she, "I thought that I was strong. I know now it was my vanity that was strong,—vanity and pride and fear, Raoul, that for a little mastered me. But in the dawn all things seem very trivial, saving love alone."

They looked out into the dew-washed gardens. The daylight was fullgrown, and already the clear-cut forms of men were passing beneath the swaying branches. In the distance a trumpet snarled.

"Dear love," said Raoul, "do you not understand that you have brought about my death? For Monsieur de Puysange is at the gates of Arnaye; and either he or Sieur Raymond will have me hanged ere noon."

"I do not know," she said, in a tired voice. "I think that Monsieur de Puysange has some cause to thank me; and my uncle loves me, and his heart, for all his gruffness, is very tender. And—see, Raoul!" She drew the dagger from her bosom. "I shall not survive you a long while, O man of all the world!"

Perplexed joy flushed through his countenance. "You will do this— for me?" he cried, with a sort of sob. "Matthiette, Matthiette, you shame me!"

"But I love you," said Matthiette. "How could it be possible, then, for me to live after you were dead?"

He bent to her. They kissed.

Hand in hand they went forth into the daylight. The kindly, familiar place seemed in Matthiette's eyes oppressed and transformed by the austerity of dawn. It was a clear Sunday morning, at the hightide of summer, and she found the world unutterably Sabbatical; only by a vigorous effort could memory connect it with the normal life of yesterday. The cool edges of the woods, vibrant now with multitudinous shrill pipings, the purple shadows shrinking eastward on the dimpling lawns, the intricate and broken traceries of the dial (where they had met so often), the blurred windings of their path, above which brooded the peaked roofs and gables and slender clerestories of Arnaye, the broad river yonder lapsing through deserted sunlit fields,—these things lay before them scarce heeded, stript of all perspective, flat as an open scroll. To them all this was alien. She and Raoul were quite apart from these matters, quite alone, despite the men of Arnaye, hurrying toward the courtyard, who stared at them curiously, but said nothing. A brisk wind was abroad in the tree-tops, scattering stray leaves, already dead, over the lush grass. Tenderly Raoul brushed a little golden sycamore leaf from the lovelier gold of Matthiette's hair.

"I do not know how long I have to live," he said. "Nobody knows that. But I wish that I might live a great while to serve you worthily."

She answered: "Neither in life nor death shall we be parted now. That only matters, my husband."

They came into the crowded court-yard just as the drawbridge fell. A troop of horse clattered into Arnaye, and the leader, a young man of frank countenance, dismounted and looked about him inquiringly. Then he came toward them.

"Monseigneur," said he, "you see that we ride early in honor of your nuptials."

Behind them some one chuckled. "Love one another, young people," said Sieur Raymond; "but do you, Matthiette, make ready to depart into Normandy as a true and faithful wife to Monsieur de Puysange."

She stared into Raoul's laughing face; there was a kind of anguish in her swift comprehension. Quickly the two men who loved her glanced at each other, half in shame.

But the Sieur d'Arnaye was not lightly dashed. "Oh, la, la, la!" chuckled the Sieur d'Arnaye, "she would never have given you a second thought, monsieur le vicomte, had I not labelled you forbidden fruit. As it is, my last conspiracy, while a little ruthless, I grant you, turns out admirably. Jack has his Jill, and all ends merrily, like an old song. I will begin on those pig-sties the first thing tomorrow morning."

"Therefore, like as May month flowereth and flourisheth in many gardens, so in likewise let every man of worship flourish his heart in this world; first unto God, and next unto the joy of them that he promiseth his faith unto."

*T*he quondam Raoul de Prison stood high in the graces of the Lady Regent of France, Anne de Beaujeu, who was, indeed, tolerably notorious for her partiality to well-built young men. Courtiers whispered more than there is any need here to rehearse. In any event, when in 1485 the daughter of Louis XI fitted out an expedition to press the Earl of Richmond's claim to the English crown, de Puysange sailed from Havre as commander of the French fleet. He fought at Bosworth, not discreditably; and a year afterward, when England had for the most part accepted Henry VII, Matthiette rejoined her husband.

They never subsequently quitted England. During the long civil wars, de Puysange was known as a shrewd captain and a judicious counsellor to the King, who rewarded his services as liberally as Tudorian parsimony would permit. After the death of Henry VII, however, the vicomte took little part in public affairs, spending most of his time at Tiverton Manor, in Devon, where, surrounded by their numerous progeny, he and Matthiette grew old together in peace and concord.

Indeed, the vicomte so ordered all his cool love-affairs that, having taken a wife as a matter of expediency, he continued as a matter of expediency to make her a fair husband, as husbands go. It also seemed to him, they relate, a matter of expediency to ignore the interpretation given by scandalous persons to the paternal friendship extended to Madame de Puysange by a high prince of the Church, during the last five years of the great Cardinal Morton's life, for the connection was useful.

The following is from a manuscript of doubtful authenticity still to be seen at Allonby Shaw. It purports to contain the autobiography of Will Sommers, the vicomte's jester, afterward court-fool to Henry VIII.

VII

The Episode Called The Castle of Content

1. *I Glimpse the Castle*

"And so, dearie," she ended, "you may seize the revenues of Allonby with unwashed hands."

I said, "Why have you done this?" I was half-frightened by the sudden whirl of Dame Fortune's wheel.

"Dear cousin in motley," grinned the beldame, "'twas for hatred of Tom Allonby and all his accursed race that I have kept the secret thus long. Now comes a braver revenge: and I settle my score with the black spawn of Allonby—euh, how entirely!—by setting you at their head."

"Nay, I elect for a more flattering reason. I begin to suspect you, cousin, of some human compunction."

"Well, Willie, well, I never hated you as much as I had reason to," she grumbled, and began to cough very lamentably. "So at the last I must make a marquis of you—ugh! Will you jest for them in counsel, Willie, and lead your henchman to battle with a bawdy song—ugh, ugh!"

Her voice crackled like burning timber, and sputtered in groans that would have been fanged curses had breath not failed her: for my aunt Elinor possessed a nimble tongue, whetted, as rumor had it, by the attendance of divers Sabbats, and the chaunting of such songs as honest men may not hear and live, however highly the succubi and warlocks and were cats, and Satan's courtiers generally, commend them.

I squinted down at one green leg, scratched the crimson fellow to it with my bauble, and could not deny that, even so, the witch was dealing handsomely with me tonight.

'Twas a strange tale which my Aunt Elinor had ended, speaking swiftly lest the worms grow impatient and Charon weigh anchor ere she had done: and the proofs of the tale's verity, set forth in a fair clerkly handwriting, rustled in my hand,—scratches of a long-rotted pen that transferred me to the right side of the blanket, and transformed the motley of a fool into the ermine of a peer.

All Devon knew I was son to Tom Allonby, who had been Marquis of Falmouth at his uncle's death, had not Tom Allonby, upon the very eve of that event, broken his neck in a fox-hunt; but Dan Gabriel, come post-haste from Heaven had with difficulty convinced the village idiot that Holy Church had smiled upon Tom's union with a tanner's daughter, and that their son was lord of Allonby Shaw. I doubted it, even as I read the proof. Yet it was true,—true that I had precedence even of the great Monsieur de Puysange, who had kept me to make him mirth on a shifty diet, first coins, then curses, these ten years past,— true that my father, rogue in all else, had yet dealt equitably with my mother ere he died,—true that my aunt, less honorably used by him, had shared their secret with the priest who married them, maliciously preserving it till this, when her words fell before me as anciently Jove's shower before the Argive Danaë, coruscant and awful, pregnant with undreamed-of chances which stirred as yet blindly in Time's womb.

A sick anger woke in me, remembering the burden of ignoble years this hag had suffered me to bear; yet my so young gentility bade me avoid reproach of the dying peasant woman, who, when all was said, had been but ill-used by our house. Death hath a strange potency: commanding as he doth, unquestioned and unchidden, the emperor to have done with slaying, the poet to rise from his unfinished rhyme, the tender and gracious lady to cease from nice denying words (mixed though they be with pitiful sighs that break their sequence like an amorous ditty heard through the strains of a martial stave), and all men, gentle or base, to follow Death's gaunt standard into unmapped realms, something of majesty enshrines the paltriest knave on whom the weight of Death's chill finger hath fallen. I doubt not that Cain's children wept about his deathbed, and that the centurions spake in whispers as they lowered Iscariot from the elder-tree: and in like manner the reproaches which stirred in my brain had no power to move my lips. The frail carnal tenement, swept and cleansed of all mortality, was garnished for Death's coming; and I could not sorrow at his advent here: but I perforce must pity rather than revile the prey which Age and Poverty, those ravenous forerunning hounds of Death yet harried, at the door of the tomb.

Running over these considerations in my mind, I said, "I forgive you."

"You posturing lack-wit!" she returned, and her sunk jaws quivered angrily. "D'ye play the condescending gentleman already! Dearie, your master did not take the news so calmly."

"You have told him?"

I had risen, for the wried, and yet sly, malice of my aunt's face was rather that of Bellona, who, as clerks avow, ever bore carnage and dissension in her train, than that of a mortal, mutton-fed woman. Elinor Sommers hated me—having God knows how just a cause—for the reason that I was my father's son; and yet, for this same reason as I think, there was in all our intercourse an odd, harsh, grudging sort of tenderness.

She laughed now,—flat and shrill, like the laughter of the damned heard in Hell between the roaring of flames. "Were it not common kindness to tell him, since this old sleek fellow's fine daughter is to wed the cuckoo that hath your nest? Yes, Willie, yes, your master hath known since morning."

"And Adeliza?" I asked, in a voice that tricked me.

"Heh, my Lady-High-and-Mighty hath, I think, heard nothing as yet. She will be hearing of new suitors soon enough, though, for her father, Monsieur Fine-Words, that silky, grinning thief, is very keen in a money-chase,—keen as a terrier on a rat-track, may Satan twist his neck! Pshutt, dearie! here is a smiling knave who means to have the estate of Allonby as it stands; what live-stock may go therewith, whether crack-brained or not, is all one to him. He will not balk at a drachm or two of wit in his son-in-law. You have but to whistle,—but to whistle, Willie, and she'll come!"

I said, "Eh, woman, and have you no heart?"

"I gave it to your father for a few lying speeches," she answered, "and Tom Allonby taught me the worth of all such commerce." There was a smile upon her lips, sister to that which Clytemnestra may have flaunted in welcome of that old Emperor Agamemnon, come in gory opulence from the sack of Troy Town. "I gave it—" Her voice rose here to a despairing wail. "Ah, go, before I lay my curse upon you, son of Thomas Allonby! But do you kiss me first, for you have just his lying mouth. So, that is better! And now go, my lord marquis; it is not fitting that death should intrude into your lordship's presence. Go, fool, and let me die in peace!"

I no longer cast a cautious eye toward the whip (ah, familiar unkindly whip!) that still hung beside the door of the hut; but, I confess, my aunt's looks were none too delectable, and ancient custom rendered her wrath yet terrible. If the farmers thereabouts were to be trusted, I knew Old Legion's bailiff would shortly be at hand, to distrain upon a soul escheat and forfeited to Dis by many years of cruel witchcrafts, close wiles, and nameless sorceries; and I could never abide unpared nails, even though they be red-hot. Therefore, I relinquished her to the village gossips, who waited without, and I tucked my bauble under my arm.

"Dear aunt," said I, "farewell!"

"Good-bye, Willie!" said she; "I shall often laugh in Hell to think of the crack-brained marquis that I made on earth. It was my will to make a beggar of Tom's son, but at the last I play the fool and cannot do it. But do you play the fool, too, dearie, and"—she chuckled here—"and have your posture and your fine long words, whatever happens."

"'Tis my vocation," I answered, briefly; and so went forth into the night.

2. *At the Ladder's Foot*

I CAME TO TIVERTON MANOR through a darkness black as the lining of Baalzebub's oldest cloak. The storm had passed, but clouds yet hung heavy as feather-beds between mankind and the stars; as I crossed the bridge the swollen Exe was but dimly visible, though it roared beneath me, and shook the frail timbers hungrily. The bridge had long been unsafe: Monsieur de Puysange had planned one stronger and less hazardous than the former edifice, of which the arches yet remained, and this was now in the making, as divers piles of unhewn lumber and stone attested: meanwhile, the roadway was a makeshift of half-rotten wood that even in this abating wind shook villainously. I stood for a moment and heard the waters lapping and splashing and laughing, as though they would hold it rare and desirable mirth to swallow and spew forth a powerful marquis, and grind his body among the battered timber and tree-boles and dead sheep swept from the hills, and at last vomit him into the sea, that a corpse, wide-eyed and livid, might bob up and down the beach, in quest of a quiet grave where the name of Allonby was scarcely known. The imagination was so vivid that it frightened me as I picked my way cat-footed through the dark.

The folk of Tiverton Manor were knotting on their nightcaps, by this; but there was a light in the Lady Adeliza's window, faint as a sick glowworm. I rolled in the seeded grass and chuckled, as I thought of what a day or two might bring about, and I murmured to myself an old cradle-song of Devon which she loved and often sang; and was, ere I knew it, carolling aloud, for pure wantonness and joy that Monsieur de

Puysange was not likely to have me whipped, now, however blatantly I might elect to discourse.

Sang I:

> "Through the mist of years does it gleam as yet—
>   That fair and free extent
>   Of moonlit turret and parapet,
>   Which castled, once, Content?
>
> "Ei ho! Ei ho! the Castle of Content,
> With drowsy music drowning merriment
> Where Dreams and Visions held high carnival,
> And frolicking frail Loves made light of all,—
> Ei ho! the vanished Castle of Content!"

As I ended, the casement was pushed open, and the Lady Adeliza came upon the balcony, the light streaming from behind her in such fashion as made her appear an angel peering out of Heaven at our mortal antics. Indeed, there was always something more than human in her loveliness, though, to be frank, it savored less of chilling paradisial perfection than of a vision of some great-eyed queen of faery, such as those whose feet glide unwetted over our fen-waters when they roam o' nights in search of unwary travellers. Lady Adeliza was a fair beauty; that is, her eyes were of the color of opals, and her complexion as the first rose of spring, blushing at her haste to snare men's hearts with beauty; and her loosened hair rippled in such a burst of splendor that I have seen a pale brilliancy, like that of amber, reflected by her bared shoulders where the bright waves fell heavily against the tender flesh, and ivory vied with gold in beauty. She was somewhat proud, they said; and to others she may have been, but to me, never. Her voice was a low, sweet song, her look that of the chaste Roman, beneficent Saint Dorothy, as she is pictured in our Chapel here at Tiverton. Proud, they called her! to me her condescensions were so manifold that I cannot set them down: indeed, in all she spoke and did there was an extreme kindliness that made a courteous word from her of more worth than a purse from another.

She said, "Is it you, Will Sommers?"

"Madonna," I answered, "with whom else should the owls confer? It is a venerable saying that extremes meet. And here you may behold it exemplified, as in the conference of an epicure and an ostrich: though, for this once, Wisdom makes bold to sit above Folly."

"Did you carol, then, to the owls of Tiverton?" she queried.

"Hand upon heart," said I, "my grim gossips care less for my melody than for the squeaking of a mouse; and I sang rather for joy that at last I may enter into the Castle of Content."

The Lady Adeliza replied, "But nobody enters there alone."

"Madonna," said I, "your apprehension is nimble. I am in hope that a woman's hand may lower the drawbridge."

She said only "You—!" Then she desisted, incredulous laughter breaking the soft flow of speech.

"Now, by Paul and Peter, those eminent apostles! the prophet Jeremy never spake more veraciously in Edom! The fool sighs for a fair woman,—what else should he do, being a fool? Ah, madonna, as in very remote times that notable jester, Love, popped out of Night's wind-egg, and by his sorcery fashioned from the primeval tangle the pleasant earth that sleeps about us,—even thus, may he not frame the disorder of a fool's brain into the semblance of a lover's? Believe me, the change is not so great as you might think. Yet if you will, laugh at me, madonna, for I love a woman far above me,—a woman who knows not of my love, or, at most, considers it but as the homage which grateful peasants accord the all-nurturing sun; so that, now chance hath woven me a ladder whereby to mount to her, I scarcely dare to set my foot upon the bottom rung."

"A ladder?" she said, oddly: "and are you talking of a rope ladder?"

"I would describe it, rather," said I, "as a golden ladder."

There came a silence. About us the wind wailed among the gaunt, deserted choir of the trees, and in the distance an owl hooted sardonically.

The Lady Adeliza said: "Be bold. Be bold, and know that a woman loves once and forever, whether she will or no. Love is not sold in the shops, and the grave merchants that trade in the ultimate seas, and send forth argosies even to jewelled Ind, to fetch home rich pearls, and strange outlandish dyes, and spiceries, and the raiment of imperious queens of the old time, have bought and sold no love, for all their traffic. It is above gold. I know"—here her voice faltered somewhat—"I know of a woman whose birth is very near the throne, and whose beauty, such as it is, hath been commended, who loved a man the politic world would have none of, for he was not rich nor famous, nor even very wise. And the world bade her relinquish him; but within the chambers of her heart his voice rang more loudly than that of the world, and for his least word said she would leave all and go with him whither he would. And—she waits only for the speaking of that word."

"Be bold?" said I.

"Ay," she returned; "that is the moral of my tale. Make me a song of it tonight, dear Will,—and tomorrow, perhaps, you may learn how this woman, too, entered into the Castle of Content."

"Madonna—!" I cried.

"It is late," said she, "and I must go."

"Tomorrow—?" I said. My heart was racing now.

"Ay, tomorrow,—the morrow that by this draws very near. Farewell!" She was gone, casting one swift glance backward, even as the ancient Parthians are fabled to have shot their arrows as they fled; and, if the airier missile, also, left a wound, I, for one, would not willingly have quitted her invulnerate.

3. *Night, and a Stormed Castle*

I WENT FORTH INTO THE woods that stand thick about Tiverton Manor, where I lay flat on my back among the fallen leaves, dreaming many dreams to myself,—dreams that were frolic songs of happiness, to which the papers in my jerkin rustled a reassuring chorus.

I have heard that night is own sister to death; now, as the ultimate torn cloud passed seaward, and the new-washed harvest-moon broke forth in a red glory, and stars clustered about her like a swarm of golden bees, I thought this night was rather the parent of a new life. But, indeed, there is a solemnity in night beyond all jesting: for night knits up the tangled yarn of our day's doings into a pattern either good or ill; it renews the vigor of the living, and with the lapsing of the tide it draws the dying toward night's impenetrable depths, gently; and it honors the secrecy of lovers as zealously as that of rogues. In the morning our bodies rise to their allotted work; but our wits have had their season in the night, or of kissing, or of junketing, or of high resolve; and the greater part of such noble deeds as day witnesses have been planned in the solitude of night. It is the sage counsellor, the potent physician that heals and comforts the sorrows of all the world: and night proved such to me, as I pondered on the proud race of Allonby, and knew that in the general record of time my name must soon be set as a sonorous word significant, as the cat might jump, for much good or for large evil.

And Adeliza loved me, and had bidden me be bold! I may not write of what my thoughts were as I considered that stupendous miracle.

But even the lark that daily soars into the naked presence of the sun must seek his woven nest among the grass at twilight; and so, with many yawns, I rose after an hour of dreams to look for sleep. Tiverton Manor was a formless blot on the mild radiance of the heavens, but I must needs pause for a while, gazing up at the Lady Adeliza's window, like a hen drinking water, and thinking of divers matters.

It was then that something rustled among the leaves, and, turning, I stared into the countenance of Stephen Allonby, until today Marquis of Falmouth, a slim, comely youth, and son to my father's younger brother.

"Fool," said he, "you walk late."

"Faith!" said I, "instinct warned me that a fool might find fit company here,—dear cousin." He frowned at the word, for he was never prone to admit the relationship, being in disposition somewhat precise.

"Eh?" said he; then paused for a while. "I have more kinsmen than I knew of," he resumed, at length, "and today spawns them thick as herrings. Your greeting falls strangely pat with that of a brother of yours, alleged to be begot in lawful matrimony, who hath appeared to claim the title and estates, and hath even imposed upon the credulity of Monsieur de Puysange."

I said, "And who is this new kinsman?" though his speaking had brought my heart into my mouth. "I have many brethren, if report speak truly as to how little my poor father slept at night."

"I do not know," said he. "The vicomte had not told me more than half the tale when I called him a double-faced old rogue. Thereafter we parted—well, rather hastily!"

I was moved with a sort of pity, since it was plainer than a pike-staff that Monsieur de Puysange had bundled this penniless young fellow out of Tiverton, with scant courtesy and a scantier explanation. Still, the wording of this sympathy was a ticklish business. I waved my hand upward. "The match, then, is broken off, between you and the Lady Adeliza?"

"Ay!" my cousin said, grimly.

Again I was nonplussed. Since their betrothal was an affair of rank conveniency, my Cousin Stephen should, in reason, grieve at this miscarriage temperately, and yet if by some awkward chance he, too, adored the delicate comeliness asleep above us, equity conceded his taste to be unfortunate rather than remarkable. Inwardly I resolved to bestow upon my Cousin Stephen a competence, and to pick out for him somewhere a wife better suited to his station. Meanwhile a silence fell.

He cleared his throat; swore softly to himself; took a brief turn on the grass; and approached me, purse in hand. "It is time you were abed," said my cousin.

I assented to this. "And since one may sleep anywhere," I reasoned, "why not here?" Thereupon, for I was somewhat puzzled at his bearing, I lay down upon the gravel and snored.

"Fool," he said. I opened one eye. "I have business here"—I opened the other—"with the Lady Adeliza." He tossed me a coin as I sprang to my feet.

"Sir—!" I cried out.

"Ho, she expects me."

"In that case—" said I.

"The difficulty is to give a signal."

"'Tis as easy as lying," I reassured him; and thereupon I began to sing. Sang I:

> *"Such toll we took of his niggling hours*
> *That the troops of Time were sent*
> *To seise the treasures and fell the towers*
> *Of the Castle of Content.*

> *"Ei ho! Ei ho! the Castle of Content,*
> *With flaming tower and tumbling battlement*
> *Where Time hath conquered, and the firelight streams*
> *Above sore-wounded Loves and dying Dreams,—*
> *Ei ho! the vanished Castle of Content!"*

And I had scarcely ended when the casement opened.

"Stephen!" said the Lady Adeliza.

"Dear love!" said he.

"Humph!" said I.

Here a rope-ladder unrolled from the balcony and hit me upon the head.

"Regard the orchard for a moment," the Lady Adeliza said, with the wonderfullest little laugh.

My cousin indignantly protested, "I have company,—a burr that sticks to me."

"A fool," I explained,—"to keep him in countenance."

"It was ever the part of folly," said she, laughing yet again, "to be swayed by a woman; and it is the part of wisdom to be discreet. In any event, there must be no spectators."

So we two Allonbys held each a strand of the ladder and stared at the ripening apples, black globes among the wind-vext silver of the leaves. In a moment the Lady Adeliza stood between us. Her hand rested upon mine as she leapt to the ground,—the tiniest velvet-soft ounce-weight that ever set a man's blood a-tingle.

"I did not know—" said she.

"Faith, madonna!" said I, "no more did I till this. I deduce but now that the Marquis of Falmouth is the person you discoursed of an hour since, with whom you hope to enter the Castle of Content."

"Ah, Will! dear Will, do not think lightly of me," she said. "My father—"

"Is as all of them have been since Father Adam's dotage," I ended; "and therefore is keeping fools and honest horses from their rest."

My cousin said, angrily, "You have been spying!"

"Because I know that there are horses yonder?" said I. "And fools here—and everywhere? Surely, there needs no argent-bearded Merlin come yawning out of Brocheliaunde to inform us of that."

He said, "You will be secret?"

"In comparison," I answered, "the grave is garrulous, and a death's-head a chattering magpie; yet I think that your maid, madonna,—"

"Beatris is sworn to silence."

"Which signifies she is already on her way to Monsieur de Puysange. She was coerced; she discovered it too late; and a sufficiency of tears and pious protestations will attest her innocence. It is all one." I winked an eye very sagely.

"Your jesting is tedious," my cousin said. "Come, Adeliza!"

Blaise, my lord marquis' French servant, held three horses in the shadow, so close that it was incredible I had not heard their trampling. Now the lovers mounted and were off like thistledown ere Blaise put foot to stirrup.

"Blaise," said I.

"Ohé!" said he, pausing.

"—if, upon this pleasurable occasion, I were to borrow your horse—"

"Impossible!"

"If I were to take it by force—" I exhibited my coin.

"Eh?"

"—no one could blame you."

"And yet perhaps—"

"The deduction is illogical," said I. And pushing him aside, I mounted and set out into the night after my cousin and the Lady Adeliza.

4. *All Ends in a Puff of Smoke*

They rode leisurely enough along the winding highway that lay in the moonlight like a white ribbon in a pedlar's box; and staying as I did some hundred yards behind, they thought me no other than Blaise, being, indeed, too much engrossed with each other to regard the outer world very strictly. So we rode a matter of three miles in the whispering, moonlit woods, they prattling and laughing as though there were no such monster in all the universe as a thrifty-minded father, and I brooding upon many things beside my marquisate, and keeping an ear cocked backward for possible pursuit.

In any ordinary falling out of affairs they would ride unhindered to Teignmouth, and thence to Allonby Shaw; they counted fully upon doing this; but I, knowing Beatris, who was waiting-maid to the Lady Adeliza, and consequently in the plot, to be the devil's own vixen, despite an innocent face and a wheedling tongue, was less certain.

I shall not easily forget that riding away from the old vicomte's preparations to make a match of it between Adeliza and me. About us the woods sighed and whispered, dappled by the moonlight with unstable chequerings of blue and silver. Tightly he clung to my crupper, that swart tireless horseman, Care; but ahead rode Love, anterior to all things and yet eternally young, in quest of the Castle of Content. The horses' hoofs beat against the pebbles as if in chorus to the Devon cradle-song that rang idly in my brain. 'Twas little to me—now—whether the quest were won or lost; yet, as I watched the Lady Adeliza's white cloak tossing and fluttering in the wind, my blood pulsed more strongly than it is wont to do, and was stirred by the keen odors of the night and by many memories of her gracious kindliness and by a desire to serve somewhat toward the attainment of her happiness. Thus it was that my teeth clenched, and a dog howled in the distance, and the world seemed very old and very incurious of our mortal woes and joys.

Then that befell which I had looked for, and I heard the clatter of horses' hoofs behind us, and knew that Monsieur de Puysange and his men were at hand to rescue the Lady Adeliza from my fine-looking young cousin, to put her into the bed of a rich fool. So I essayed a gallop.

"Spur!" I cried;—"in the name of Saint Cupid!"

With a little gasp, she bent forward over her horse's mane, urging him onward with every nerve and muscle of her tender body. I could not keep my gaze from her as we swept through the night. Picture Europa in her traverse, bull-borne, through the summer sea, the depths giving up their misshapen deities, and the blind sea-snakes writhing about her in hideous homage, while she, a little frightened, thinks resolutely of Crete beyond these unaccustomed horrors and of the god desirous of her contentation; and there, to an eyelash, you have Adeliza as I saw her.

But steadily our pursuers gained on us: and as we paused to pick our way over the frail bridge that spanned the Exe, their clamor was very near.

"Take care!" I cried,—but too late, for my horse swerved under me as I spoke, and my lord marquis' steed caught foot in a pile of lumber and fell heavily. He was up in a moment, unhurt, but the horse was lamed.

"You!" cried my Cousin Stephen. "Oh, but what fiend sends me this burr again!"

I said: "My fellow-madmen, it is all one if I have a taste for night-riding and the shedding of noble blood. Alack, though, that I have left my brave bauble at Tiverton! Had I that here, I might do such deeds! I might show such prowess upon the person of Monsieur de Puysange as your Nine Worthies would quake to hear of! For I have the honor to inform you, my doves, that we are captured."

Indeed, we were in train to be, for even the two sound horses were well-nigh foundered: Blaise, the idle rogue, had not troubled to provide fresh steeds, so easy had the flitting seemed; and it was conspicuous that we would be overtaken in half an hour.

"So it seems," said Stephen Allonby. "Well! one can die but once." Thus speaking, he drew his sword with an air which might have been envied by Captain Leonidas at Thermopylae.

"Together, my heart!" she cried.

"Madonna," said I, dismounting as I spoke, "pray you consider! With neither of you, is there any question of death; 'tis but that Monsieur de Puysange desires you to make a suitable match. It is not yet too late; his heart is kindly so long as he gets his will and profit everywhere, and he bears no malice toward my lord marquis. Yield, then, to your father's wishes, since there is no choice."

She stared at me, as thanks for this sensible advice. "And you—is it you that would enter into the Castle of Content?" she cried, with a scorn that lashed.

I said: "Madonna, bethink you, you know naught of this man your father desires you to wed. Is it not possible that he, too, may love—or may learn to love you, on provocation? You are very fair, madonna. Yours is a beauty that may draw a man to Heaven or unclose the gates of Hell, at will; indeed, even I, in my poor dreams, have seen your face as bright and glorious as is the lighted space above the altar when Christ's blood and body are shared among His worshippers. Men certainly will never cease to love you. Will he—your husband that may be—prove less susceptible, we will say, than I? Ah, but, madonna, let us unrein imagination! Suppose, were it possible, that he—even now—yearns to enter into the Castle of Content, and that your hand, your hand alone, may draw the bolt for him,—that the thought of you is to him as a flame before which honor and faith shrivel as shed feathers, and that he has loved you these many years, unknown to you, long, long before the Marquis of Falmouth came into your life with his fair face and smooth sayings. Suppose, were it possible, that he now stood before you, every pulse and fibre of him racked with an intolerable ecstasy of loving you, his heart one vast hunger for you, Adeliza, and his voice shaking as my voice shakes, and his hands trembling as my hands tremble,—ah, see how they tremble, madonna, the poor foolish hands! Suppose, were it possible,—"

"Fool! O treacherous fool!" my cousin cried, in a fine rage.

She rested her finger-tips upon his arm. "Hush!" she bade him; then turned to me an uncertain countenance that was half pity, half wonder. "Dear Will," said she, "if you have ever known aught of love, do you not understand how I love Stephen here?"

But she did not any longer speak as a lord's daughter speaks to the fool that makes mirth for his betters.

"In that case," said I,—and my voice played tricks,—"in that case, may I request that you assist me in gathering such brushwood as we may find hereabout?"

They both stared at me now. "My lord," I said, "the Exe is high, the bridge is of wood, and I have flint and steel in my pocket. The ford is five miles above and quite impassable. Do you understand me, my lord?"

He clapped his hands. "Oh, excellent!" he cried.

Then, each having caught my drift, we heaped up a pile of broken boughs and twigs and brushwood on the bridge, all three gathering it together. And I wondered if the moon, that is co-partner in the antics of most rogues and lovers, had often beheld a sight more reasonless than the foregathering of a marquis, a peer's daughter, and a fool at dead of night to make fagots.

When we had done I handed him the flint and steel. "My lord," said I, "the honor is yours."

"Udsfoot!" he murmured, in a moment, swearing and striking futile sparks, "but the late rain has so wet the wood that it will not kindle."

I said, "Assuredly, in such matters a fool is indispensable." I heaped before him the papers that made an honest woman of my mother and a marquis of me, and seizing the flint, I cast a spark among them that set them crackling cheerily. Oh, I knew well enough that patience would coax a flame from those twigs without my paper's aid, but to be patient does not afford the posturing which youth loves. So it was a comfort to wreck all magnificently: and I knew that, too, as we three drew back upon the western bank and watched the writhing twigs splutter and snap and burn.

The bridge caught apace and in five minutes afforded passage to nothing short of the ardent equipage of the prophet Elias. Five minutes later the bridge did not exist: only the stone arches towered above the roaring waters that glistened in the light of the fire, which had, by this, reached the other side of the river, to find quick employment in the woods of Tiverton. Our pursuers rode through a glare which was that of Hell's kitchen on baking-day, and so reached the Exe only to curse vainly and to shriek idle imprecations at us, who were as immune from their anger as though the severing river had been Pyriphlegethon.

"My lord," I presently suggested, "it may be that your priest expects you?"

"Indeed," said he, laughing, "it is possible. Let us go." Thereupon they mounted the two sound horses. "Most useful burr," said he, "do you follow on foot to Teignmouth; and there—"

"Sir," I replied, "my home is at Tiverton."

He wheeled about. "Do you not fear—?"

"The whip?" said I. "Ah, my lord, I have been whipped ere this. It is not the greatest ill in life to be whipped."

He began to protest.

"But, indeed, I am resolved," said I. "Farewell!"

He tossed me his purse. "As you will," he retorted, shortly. "We thank you for your aid; and if I am still master of Allonby—"

"No fear of that!" I said. "Farewell, good cousin marquis! I cannot weep at your going, since it brings you happiness. And we have it on excellent authority that the laughter of fools is as the crackling of thorns under a pot. Accordingly, I bid you God-speed in a discreet silence."

I stood fumbling my cousin's gold as he went forward into the night; but she did not follow.

"I am sorry—" she began. She paused and the lithe fingers fretted with her horse's mane.

I said: "Madonna, earlier in this crowded night, you told me of love's nature: must my halting commentary prove the glose upon your text? Look, then, to be edified while the fool is delivered of his folly. For upon the maternal side, love was born of the ocean, madonna, and the ocean is but salt water, and salt water is but tears; and thus may love claim love's authentic kin with sorrow. Ay, certainly, madonna, Fate hath ordained for her diversion that through sorrow alone we lovers may attain to the true Castle of Content."

There was a long silence, and the wind wailed among the falling, tattered leaves. "Had I but known—" said Adeliza, very sadly.

I said: "Madonna, go forward and God speed you! Yonder your lover waits for you, and the world is exceedingly fair; here is only a fool. As for this new Marquis of Falmouth, let him trouble you no longer. 'Tis an Eastern superstition that we lackbrains are endowed with peculiar gifts of prophecy: and as such, I predict, very confidently, madonna, that you will see and hear no more of him in this life."

I caught my breath. In the moonlight she seemed God's masterwork. Her eyes were big with half-comprehended sorrow, and a slender hand stole timorously toward me. I laughed, seeing how she strove to pity my great sorrow and could not, by reason of her great happiness. I laughed and was content. "As surely as God reigns in Heaven," I cried aloud, "I am content, and this moment is well purchased with a marquisate!"

Indeed, I was vastly uplift and vastly pleased with my own nobleness, just then, and that condition is always a comfort.

More alertly she regarded me; and in her eyes I saw the anxiety and the wonder merge now into illimitable pity. "That, too!" she said, smiling sadly. "That, too, O son of Thomas Allonby!" And her mothering arms were clasped about me, and her lips clung and were one with my lips for a moment, and her tears were wet upon my cheek. She seemed to shield me, making of her breast my sanctuary.

"My dear, my dear, I am not worthy!" said Adeliza, with a tenderness I cannot tell you of; and presently she, too, was gone.

I mounted the lamed horse, who limped slowly up the river bank; very slowly we came out from the glare of the crackling fire into the cool darkness of the autumn woods; very slowly, for the horse was lamed and wearied, and patience is a discreet virtue when one journeys toward curses and the lash of a dog-whip: and I thought of many quips and jests whereby to soothe the anger of Monsieur de Puysange, and I sang to myself as I rode through the woods, a nobleman no longer, a tired Jack-pudding whose tongue must save his hide.

Sang I:

> *"The towers are fallen; no laughter rings*
> *Through the rafters, charred and rent;*
> *The ruin is wrought of all goodly things*
> *In the Castle of Content.*

> *"Ei ho! Ei ho! the Castle of Content,*
> *Rased in the Land of Youth, where mirth was meant!*
> *Nay, all is ashes there; and all in vain*
> *Hand-shadowed eyes turn backward, to regain*
> *Disastrous memories of that dear domain,—*
> *Ei ho! the vanished Castle of Content!"*

MAY 27, 1559

"'O welladay!' said Beichan then,
'That I so soon have married thee!
For it can be none but Susie Pie,
That sailed the sea for love of me.'"

*H*ow Will Sommers encountered the Marchioness of Falmouth in the Cardinal's house at Whitehall, and how in Windsor Forest that noble lady died with the fool's arms about her, does not concern us here. That is matter for another tale.

You are not, though, to imagine any scandal. Barring an affair with Sir Henry Rochford, and another with Lord Norreys, and the brief interval in 1525 when the King was enamored of her, there is no record that the marchioness ever wavered from the choice her heart had made, or had any especial reason to regret it.

So she lived and died, more virtuously and happily than most, and found the marquis a fair husband, as husbands go; and bore him three sons and a daughter.

But when the ninth Marquis of Falmouth died long after his wife, in the November of 1557, he was survived by only one of these sons, a junior Stephen, born in 1530, who at his father's demise succeeded to the title. The oldest son, Thomas, born 1531, had been killed in Wyatt's Rebellion in 1554; the second, George, born 1526, with a marked look of the King, was, in February, 1556, stabbed in a disreputable tavern brawl.

Now we have to do with the tenth Marquis of Falmouth's suit for the hand of Lady Ursula Heleigh, the Earl of Brudenel's co-heiress. You are to imagine yourself at Longaville Court, in Sussex, at a time when Anne Bullen's daughter was very recently become Queen of England.

VIII

The Episode Called In Ursula's Garden

1. Love, and Love's Mimic

Her three lovers had praised her with many canzonets and sonnets on that May morning as they sat in the rose-garden at Longaville, and the sun-steeped leaves made a tempered aromatic shade about them. Afterward they had drawn grass-blades to decide who should accompany the Lady Ursula to the summer pavilion, that she might fetch her viol and sing them a song of love, and in the sylvan lottery chance had favored the Earl of Pevensey.

Left to themselves, the Marquis of Falmouth and Master Richard Mervale regarded each the other, irresolutely, like strange curs uncertain whether to fraternize or to fly at one another's throat. Then Master Mervale lay down in the young grass, stretched himself, twirled his thin black mustachios, and chuckled in luxurious content.

"Decidedly," said he, "your lordship is past master in the art of wooing; no university in the world would refuse you a degree."

The marquis frowned. He was a great bluff man, with wheat-colored hair, and was somewhat slow-witted. After a little he found the quizzical, boyish face that mocked him irresistible, and he laughed, and unbent from the dignified reserve which he had for a while maintained portentously.

"Master Mervale," said the marquis, "I will be frank with you, for you appear a lad of good intelligence, as lads run, and barring a trifle of affectation and a certain squeamishness in speech. When I would go exploring into a woman's heart, I must pay my way in the land's current coinage of compliments and high-pitched protestations. Yes, yes, such sixpenny phrases suffice the seasoned traveler, who does not ostentatiously display his gems while traveling. Now, in courtship, Master Mervale, one traverses ground more dubious than the Indies, and the truth, Master Mervale, is a jewel of great price."

Master Mervale raised his eyebrows. "The truth?" he queried, gently. "Now how, I wonder, did your lordship happen to think of that remote abstraction." For beyond doubt, Lord Falmouth's wooing had been that morning of a rather florid sort.

However, "It would surely be indelicate," the marquis suggested, "to allow even truth to appear quite unclothed in the presence of a lady?" He smiled and took a short turn on the grass. "Look you, Master Mervale," said he, narrowing his pale-blue eyes to slits, "I have, somehow, a disposition to confidence come upon me. Frankly, my passion for the Lady Ursula burns more mildly than that which Antony bore the Egyptian; it is less a fire to consume kingdoms than a candle wherewith to light a contented home; and quite frankly, I mean to have her. The estates lie convenient, the families are of equal rank, her father is agreed, and she has a sufficiency of beauty; there are, in short, no obstacles to our union save you and my lord of Pevensey, and these, I confess, I do not fear. I can wait, Master Mervale. Oh, I am patient, Master Mervale, but, I own, I cannot brook denial. It is I, or no one. By Saint Gregory! I wear steel at my side, Master Mervale, that will serve for other purposes save that of opening oysters!" So he blustered in the spring sunlight, and frowned darkly when Master Mervale appeared the more amused than impressed.

"Your patience shames Job the Patriarch," said Master Mervale, "yet, it seems to me, my lord, you do not consider one thing. I grant you that Pevensey and I are your equals neither in estate nor reputation; still, setting modesty aside, is it not possible the Lady Ursula may come, in time, to love one of us?"

"Setting common sense aside," said the marquis, stiffly, "it is possible she may be smitten with the smallpox. Let us hope, however, that she may escape both of these misfortunes."

The younger man refrained from speech for a while. Presently, "You liken love to a plague," he said, "yet I have heard there was once a cousin of the Lady Ursula's—a Mistress Katherine Beaufort—"

"Swounds!" Lord Falmouth had wheeled about, scowled, and then tapped sharply upon the palm of one hand with the nail-bitten fingers of the other. "Ay," said he, more slowly, "there was such a person."

"She loved you?" Master Mervale suggested.

"God help me!" replied the marquis; "we loved each other! I know not how you came by your information, nor do I ask. Yet, it is ill to open an old wound. I loved her; let that suffice." With a set face, he turned away for a moment and gazed toward the high parapets of Longaville, half-hidden by pale foliage and very white against the rain-washed sky; then groaned, and glared angrily into the lad's upturned countenance. "You talk of love," said the marquis; "a love compounded equally of youthful imagination, a liking for fantastic phrases and a disposition for caterwauling i' the moonlight. Ah, lad, lad!—if you but knew! That is not love; to love is to go mad like a star-struck moth, and afterward to strive in vain to forget, and to eat one's heart out in the loneliness, and to hunger—hunger—" The marquis spread his big hands helplessly, and then, with a quick, impatient gesture, swept back the mass of wheat-colored hair that fell about his face. "Ah, Master Mervale," he sighed, "I was right after all,—it is the cruelest plague in the world, and that same smallpox leaves less troubling scars."

"Yet," Master Mervale said, with courteous interest, "you did not marry?"

"Marry!" His lordship snarled toward the sun and laughed. "Look you, Master Mervale, I know not how far y'are acquainted with the business. It was in Cornwall yonder years since; I was but a lad, and she a wench,—Oh, such a wench, with tender blue eyes, and a faint, sweet voice that could deny me nothing! God does not fashion her like every day,—*Dieu qui la fist de ses deux mains*, saith the Frenchman." The marquis paced the grass, gnawing his lip and debating with himself. "Marry? Her family was good, but their deserts outranked their fortunes; their crest was not the topmost feather in Fortune's cap, you understand; somewhat sunken i' the world, Master Mervale, somewhat sunken. And I? My father—God rest his bones!—was a cold, hard man, and my two elder brothers—Holy Virgin, pray for them!—loved me none too well. I was the cadet then: Heaven helps them that help themselves, says my father, and I ha'n't a penny for you. My way was yet to make in the world; to saddle myself with a dowerless wench—even a wench whose least 'Good-morning' set a man's heart hammering at his ribs—would have been folly, Master Mervale. Utter, improvident, shiftless, bedlamite folly, lad!"

"H'm!" Master Mervale cleared his throat, twirled his mustachios, and smiled at some unspoken thought. "We pay for our follies in this world, my lord, but I sometimes think that we pay even more dearly for our wisdom."

"Ah, lad, lad!" the marquis cried, in a gust of anger; "I dare say, as your smirking hints, it was a coward's act not to snap fingers at fate and fathers and dare all! Well! I did not dare. We parted—in what lamentable fashion is now of little import—and I set forth to seek my fortune. Ho, it was a brave world then, Master Mervale, for all the tears that were scarce dried on my cheeks! A world wherein the heavens were as blue as a certain woman's eyes,—a world wherein a likely lad might see far countries, waggle a good sword in Babylon and Tripolis and other ultimate kingdoms, beard the Mussulman in his mosque, and at last fetch home—though he might never love her, you understand—a soldan's daughter for his wife,—

> *With more gay gold about her middle*
> *Than would buy half Northumberlee."*

His voice died away. He sighed and shrugged. "Eh, well!" said the marquis; "I fought in Flanders somewhat—in Spain—what matter where? Then, at last, sickened in Amsterdam, three years ago, where a messenger comes to haul me out of bed as future Marquis of Falmouth. One brother slain in a duel, Master Mervale; one killed in Wyatt's Rebellion; my father dying, and—Heaven rest his soul!—not over-eager to meet his Maker. There you have it, Master Mervale,—a right pleasant jest of Fortune's perpetration,—I a marquis, my own master, fit mate for any woman in the kingdom, and Kate—my Kate who was past human praising!—vanished."

"Vanished?" The lad echoed the word, with wide eyes.

"Vanished in the night, and no sign nor rumor of her since! Gone to seek me abroad, no doubt, poor wench! Dead, dead, beyond question, Master Mervale!" The marquis swallowed, and rubbed his lips with the back of his hand. "Ah, well!" said he; "it is an old sorrow!"

The male animal shaken by strong emotion is to his brothers an embarrassing rather than a pathetic sight. Master Mervale, lowering his eyes discreetly, rooted up several tufts of grass before he spoke. Then, "My lord, you have known of love," said he, very slowly; "does there survive no kindliness for aspiring lovers in you who have been one of us? My lord of Pevensey, I think, loves the Lady Ursula, at least, as much as you ever loved this Mistress Katherine; of my own adoration I do not speak, save to say that I have sworn never to marry any other woman. Her father favors you, for you are a match in a thousand; but you do not love her. It matters little to you, my lord, whom she may wed; to us it signifies a life's happiness. Will not the memory of that Cornish lass—the memory of moonlit nights, and of those sweet, vain aspirations and foiled day-dreams that in boyhood waked your blood even to such brave folly as now possesses us,—will not the memory of these things soften you, my lord?"

But Falmouth by this time appeared half regretful of his recent outburst, and somewhat inclined to regard his companion as a dangerously plausible young fellow who had very unwarrantably wormed himself into Lord Falmouth's confidence. Falmouth's heavy jaw shut like a trap.

"By Saint Gregory!" said he; "if ever such notions soften me at all, I pray to be in hell entirely melted! What I have told you of is past, Master Mervale; and a wise man does not meditate unthriftily upon spilt milk."

"You are adamant?" sighed the boy.

"The nether millstone," said the marquis, smiling grimly, "is in comparison a pillow of down."

"Yet—yet the milk was sweet, my lord?" the boy suggested, with a faint answering smile.

"Sweet!" The marquis' voice had a deep tremor.

"And if the choice lay between Ursula and Katherine?"

"Oh, fool!—Oh, pink-cheeked, utter ignorant fool!" the marquis groaned. "Did I not say you knew nothing of love?"

"Heigho!" Master Mervale put aside all glum-faced discussion, with a little yawn, and sprang to his feet. "Then we can but hope that somewhere, somehow, Mistress Katherine yet lives and in her own good time may reappear. And while we speak of reappearances—surely the Lady Ursula is strangely tardy in making hers?"

The marquis' jealousy when it slumbered slept with an open ear. "Let us join them," he said, shortly, and he started through the gardens with quick, stiff strides.

2. *Song-guerdon*

THEY WENT WESTWARD TOWARD THE summer pavilion. Presently the marquis blundered into the green gloom of the maze, laid out in the Italian fashion, and was extricated only by the superior knowledge of Master Mervale, who guided Falmouth skilfully and surely through manifold intricacies, to open daylight.

Afterward they came to a close-shaven lawn, where the summer pavilion stood beside the brook that widened here into an artificial pond, spread with lily-pads and fringed with rushes. The Lady Ursula sat with the Earl of Pevensey beneath a burgeoning maple-tree. Such rays as sifted through into their cool retreat lay like splotches of wine upon the ground, and there the taller grass-blades turned to needles of thin silver; one palpitating beam, more daring than the rest, slanted straight toward the little head of the Lady Ursula, converting her hair into a halo of misty gold, that appeared out of place in this particular position. She seemed a Bassarid who had somehow fallen heir to an aureole; for otherwise, to phrase it sedately, there was about her no clamant suggestion of saintship. At least, there is no record of any saint in the calendar who ever looked with laughing gray-green eyes upon her lover and mocked at the fervor and trepidation of his speech. This the Lady Ursula now did; and, manifestly, enjoyed the doing of it.

Within the moment the Earl of Pevensey took up the viol that lay beside them, and sang to her in the clear morning. He was sunbrowned and very comely, and his big, black eyes were tender as he sang to her sitting there in the shade. He himself sat at her feet in the sunlight.

Sang the Earl of Pevensey:

> *"Ursula, spring wakes about us—*
> *Wakes to mock at us and flout us*
> *That so coldly do delay:*
> *When the very birds are mating,*
> *Pray you, why should we be waiting—*
> *We that might be wed today!*
>
> *"'Life is short,' the wise men tell us;—*
> *Even those dusty, musty fellows*
> *That have done with life,—and pass*
> *Where the wraith of Aristotle*
> *Hankers, vainly, for a bottle,*
> *Youth and some frank Grecian lass.*
>
> *"Ah, I warrant you;—and Zeno*
> *Would not reason, now, could he know*
> *One more chance to live and love:*
> *For, at best, the merry May-time*
> *Is a very fleeting play-time;—*
> *Why, then, waste an hour thereof?*
>
> *"Plato, Solon, Periander,*
> *Seneca, Anaximander,*

Pyrrho, and Parmenides!
Were one hour alone remaining
Would ye spend it in attaining
Learning, or to lips like these?

"Thus, I demonstrate by reason
Now is our predestined season
For the garnering of all bliss;
Prudence is but long-faced folly;
Cry a fig for melancholy!
Seal the bargain with a kiss"

When he had ended, the Earl of Pevensey laughed and looked up into the Lady Ursula's face with a long, hungry gaze; and the Lady Ursula laughed likewise and spoke kindly to him, though the distance was too great for the eavesdroppers to overhear. Then, after a little, the Lady Ursula bent forward, out of the shade of the maple into the sun, so that the sunlight fell upon her golden head and glowed in the depths of her hair, as she kissed Pevensey, tenderly and without haste, full upon the lips.

3. *Falmouth Furens*

THE MARQUIS OF FALMOUTH CAUGHT Master Mervale's arm in a grip that made the boy wince. Lord Falmouth's look was murderous, as he turned in the shadow of a white-lilac bush and spoke carefully through sharp breaths that shook his great body.

"There are," said he, "certain matters I must immediately discuss with my lord of Pevensey. I desire you, Master Mervale, to fetch him to the spot where we parted last, so that we may talk over these matters quietly and undisturbed. For else—go, lad, and fetch him!"

For a moment the boy faced the half-shut pale eyes that were like coals smouldering behind a veil of gray ash. Then he shrugged his shoulders, sauntered forward, and doffed his hat to the Lady Ursula. There followed much laughter among the three, many explanations from Master Mervale, and yet more laughter from the lady and the earl. The marquis ground his big, white teeth as he listened, and he appeared to disapprove of so much mirth.

"Foh, the hyenas! the apes, the vile magpies!" the marquis observed. He heaved a sigh of relief, as the Earl of Pevensey, raising his hands lightly toward heaven, laughed once more, and departed into the thicket. Lord Falmouth laughed in turn, though not very pleasantly. Afterward he loosened his sword in the scabbard and wheeled back to seek their rendezvous in the shadowed place where they had made sonnets to the Lady Ursula.

For some ten minutes the marquis strode proudly through the maze, pondering, by the look of him, on the more fatal tricks of fencing. In a quarter of an hour he was lost in a wilderness of trim yew-hedges which confronted him stiffly at every outlet and branched off into innumerable gravelled alleys that led nowhither.

"Swounds!" said the marquis. He retraced his steps impatiently. He cast his hat upon the ground in seething desperation. He turned in a different direction, and in two minutes trod upon his discarded headgear.

"Holy Gregory!" the marquis commented. He meditated for a moment, then caught up his sword close to his side and plunged into the nearest hedge. After a little he came out, with a scratched face and a scant breath, into another alley. As the crow flies, he went through the maze of Longaville, leaving in his rear desolation and snapped yew-twigs. He came out of the ruin behind the white-lilac bush, where he had stood and had heard the Earl of Pevensey sing to the Lady Ursula, and had seen what followed.

The marquis wiped his brow. He looked out over the lawn and breathed heavily. The Lady Ursula still sat beneath the maple, and beside her was Master Mervale, whose arm girdled her waist. Her arm was about his neck, and she listened as he talked eagerly with many gestures. Then they both laughed and kissed each other.

"Oh, defend me!" groaned the marquis. Once more he wiped his brow, as he crouched behind the white-lilac bush. "Why, the woman is a second Messalina!" he said. "Oh, the trollop! the wanton! Oh, holy Gregory! Yet I must be quiet—quiet as a sucking lamb, that I may strike afterward as a roaring lion. Is this your innocence, Mistress Ursula, that cannot endure the spoken name of a spade? Oh, splendor of God!"

Thus he raged behind the white-lilac bush while they laughed and kissed under the maple-tree. After a space they parted. The Lady Ursula, still laughing, lifted the branches of the rearward thicket and disappeared in the path which the Earl of Pevensey had taken. Master Mervale, kissing his hand and laughing yet more loudly, lounged toward the entrance of the maze.

The jackanapes (as anybody could see), was in a mood to be pleased with himself. Smiles eddied about the boy's face, his heels skipped, disdaining the honest grass; and presently he broke into a glad little song, all trills and shakes, like that of a bird ecstasizing over the perfections of his mate.

Sang Master Mervale:

> *"Listen, all lovers! the spring is here*
> *And the world is not amiss;*
> *As long as laughter is good to hear,*
> *And lips are good to kiss,*
> *As long as Youth and Spring endure,*
> *There is never an evil past a cure*
> *And the world is never amiss.*
>
> *"O lovers all, I bid ye declare*
> *The world is a pleasant place;—*
> *Give thanks to God for the gift so fair,*
> *Give thanks for His singular grace!*
> *Give thanks for Youth and Love and Spring!*
> *Give thanks, as gentlefolk should, and sing,*
> *'The world is a pleasant place!'"*

In mid-skip Master Mervale here desisted, his voice trailing into inarticulate vowels. After many angry throes, a white-lilac bush had been delivered of the Marquis of Falmouth, who now confronted Master Mervale, furiously moved.

4. *Love Rises from un-Cytherean Waters*

"I HAVE HEARD, MASTER MERVALE," said the marquis, gently, "that love is blind?"

The boy stared at the white face, that had before his eyes veiled rage with a crooked smile. So you may see the cat, tense for the fatal spring, relax and with one paw indolently flip the mouse.

"It is an ancient fable, my lord," the boy said, smiling, and made as though to pass.

"Indeed," said the marquis, courteously, but without yielding an inch, "it is a very reassuring fable: for," he continued, meditatively, "were the eyes of all lovers suddenly opened, Master Mervale, I suspect it would prove a red hour for the world. There would be both tempers and reputations lost, Master Mervale; there would be sword-thrusts; there would be corpses, Master Mervale."

"Doubtless, my lord," the lad assented, striving to jest and have done; "for all flesh is frail, and as the flesh of woman is frailer than that of man, so is it, as I remember to have read, the more easily entrapped by the gross snares of the devil, as was over-well proved by the serpent's beguiling deceit of Eve at the beginning."

"Yet, Master Mervale," pursued the marquis, equably, but without smiling, "there be lovers in the world that have eyes?"

"Doubtless, my lord," said the boy.

"There also be women in the world, Master Mervale," Lord Falmouth suggested, with a deeper gravity, "that are but the handsome sepulchres of iniquity,—ay, and for the major part of women, those miracles which are their bodies, compact of white and gold and sprightly color though they be, serve as the lovely cerements of corruption."

"Doubtless, my lord. The devil, as they say, is homelier with that sex."

"There also be swords in the world, Master Mervale?" purred the marquis. He touched his own sword as he spoke.

"My lord—!" the boy cried, with a gasp.

"Now, swords have at least three uses, Master Mervale," Falmouth continued. "With a sword one may pick a cork from a bottle; with a sword one may toast cheese about the Twelfth Night fire; and with a sword one may spit a man, Master Mervale,—ay, even an ambling, pink-faced, lisping lad that cannot boo at a goose, Master Mervale. I have no inclination, Master Mervale, just now, for either wine or toasted cheese."

"I do not understand you, my lord," said the boy, in a thin voice.

"Indeed, I think we understand each other perfectly," said the marquis. "For I have been very frank with you, and I have watched you from behind this bush."

The boy raised his hand as though to speak.

"Look you, Master Mervale," the marquis argued, "you and my lord of Pevensey and I be brave fellows; we need a wide world to bustle in. Now, the thought has come to me that this small planet of ours is scarcely commodious enough for all three. There be purgatory and Heaven, and yet another place, Master Mervale; why, then, crowd one another?"

"My lord," said the boy, dully, "I do not understand you."

"Holy Gregory!" scoffed the marquis; "surely my meaning is plain enough! it is to kill you first, and my lord of Pevensey afterward! Y'are phoenixes, Master Mervale, Arabian birds! Y'are too good for this world. Longaville is not fit to be trodden under your feet; and therefore it is my intention that you leave Longaville feet first. Draw, Master Mervale!" cried the marquis, his light hair falling about his flushed, handsome face as he laughed joyously, and flashed his sword in the spring sunshine.

The boy sprang back, with an inarticulate cry; then gulped some dignity into himself and spoke. "My lord," he said, "I admit that explanation may seem necessary."

"You will render it, if to anybody, Master Mervale, to my heir, who will doubtless accord it such credence as it merits. For my part, having two duels on my hands today, I have no time to listen to a romance out of the Hundred Merry Tales."

Falmouth had placed himself on guard; but Master Mervale stood with chattering teeth and irresolute, groping hands, and made no effort to draw. "Oh, the block! the curd-faced cheat!" cried the marquis. "Will nothing move you?" With his left hand he struck at the boy.

Thereupon Master Mervale gasped, and turning with a great sob, ran through the gardens. The marquis laughed discordantly; then he followed, taking big leaps as he ran and flourishing his sword.

"Oh, the coward!" he shouted; "Oh, the milk-livered rogue! Oh, you paltry rabbit!"

So they came to the bank of the artificial pond. Master Mervale swerved as with an oath the marquis pounced at him. Master Mervale's foot caught in the root of a great willow, and Master Mervale splashed into ten feet of still water, that glistened like quicksilver in the sunlight.

"Oh, Saint Gregory!" the marquis cried, and clasped his sides in noisy mirth; "was there no other way to cool your courage? Paddle out and be flogged, Master Hare-heels!" he called. The boy had come to the surface and was swimming aimlessly, parallel to the bank. "Now I have heard," said the marquis, as he walked beside him, "that water swells a man. Pray Heaven, it may swell his heart a thousandfold or so, and thus hearten him for wholesome exercise after his ducking—a friendly thrust or two, a little judicious bloodletting to ward off the effects of the damp."

The marquis started as Master Mervale grounded on a shallow and rose, dripping, knee-deep among the lily-pads. "Oh, splendor of God!" cried the marquis.

Master Mervale had risen from his bath almost clean-shaven; only one sodden half of his mustachios clung to his upper lip, and as he rubbed the water from his eyes, this remaining half also fell away from the boy's face.

"Oh, splendor of God!" groaned the marquis. He splashed noisily into the water. "O Kate, Kate!" he cried, his arms about Master Mervale. "Oh, blind, blind, blind! O heart's dearest! Oh, my dear, my dear!" he observed.

Master Mervale slipped from his embrace and waded to dry land. "My lord,—" he began, demurely.

"My lady wife,—" said his lordship of Falmouth, with a tremulous smile. He paused, and passed his hand over his brow. "And yet I do not understand," he said. "Y'are dead; y'are buried. It was a frightened boy I struck." He spread out his strong arms. "O world! O sun! O stars!" he cried; "she is come back to me from the grave. O little world! small shining planet! I think that I could crush you in my hands!"

"Meanwhile," Master Mervale suggested, after an interval, "it is I that you are crushing." He sighed,—though not very deeply,—and continued, with a hiatus: "They would have wedded me to Lucius Rossmore, and I could not—I could not—"

"That skinflint! that palsied goat!" the marquis growled.

"He was wealthy," said Master Mervale. Then he sighed once more. "There seemed only you,—only you in all the world. A man might come to you in those far-off countries: a woman might not. I fled by night, my lord, by the aid of a waiting-woman; became a man by the aid of a tailor; and set out to find you by the aid of such impudence as I might muster. But luck did not travel with me. I followed you through Flanders, Italy, Spain,—always just too late; always finding the bird flown, the nest yet warm. Presently I heard you were become Marquis of Falmouth; then I gave up the quest."

"I would suggest," said the marquis, "that my name is Stephen;—but why, in the devil's name, should you give up a quest so laudable?"

"Stephen Allonby, my lord," said Master Mervale, sadly, "was not Marquis of Falmouth; as Marquis of Falmouth, you might look to mate with any woman short of the Queen."

"To tell you a secret," the marquis whispered, "I look to mate with one beside whom the Queen—not to speak treason—is but a lean-faced, yellow piece of affectation. I aim higher than royalty, heart's dearest,—aspiring to one beside whom empresses are but common hussies."

"And Ursula?" asked Master Mervale, gently.

"Holy Gregory!" cried the marquis, "I had forgot! Poor wench, poor wench! I must withdraw my suit warily,—firmly, of course, yet very kindlily, you understand, so as to grieve her no more than must be. Poor wench!—well, after all," he hopefully suggested, "there is yet Pevensey."

"O Stephen! Stephen!" Master Mervale murmured; "Why, there was never any other but Pevensey! For Ursula knows all,—knows there was never any more manhood in Master Mervale's disposition than might be gummed on with a play-actor's mustachios! Why, she is my cousin, Stephen,—my cousin and good friend, to whom I came at once on reaching England, to find you, favored by her father, pestering her with your suit, and the poor girl well-nigh at her wits' end because she might not have Pevensey. So," said Master Mervale, "we put our heads together, Stephen, as you observe."

"Indeed," my lord of Falmouth said, "it would seem that you two wenches have, between you, concocted a very pleasant comedy."

"It was not all a comedy," sighed Master Mervale,—"not all a comedy, Stephen, until today when you told Master Mervale the story of Katherine Beaufort. For I did not know—I could not know—"

"And now?" my lord of Falmouth queried.

"H'm!" cried Master Mervale, and he tossed his head. "You are very unreasonable in anger! you are a veritable Turk! you struck me!"

The marquis rose, bowing low to his former adversary. "Master Mervale," said the marquis, "I hereby tender you my unreserved apologies for the affront I put upon you. I protest I was vastly mistaken in your disposition and hold you as valorous a gentleman as was ever made by barbers' tricks; and you are at liberty to bestow as many kisses and caresses upon the Lady Ursula as you may elect, reserving, however, a reasonable sufficiency for one that shall be nameless. Are we friends, Master Mervale?"

Master Mervale rested his head upon Lord Falmouth's shoulder, and sighed happily. Master Mervale laughed,—a low and gentle laugh that was vibrant with content. But Master Mervale said nothing, because there seemed to be between these two, who were young in the world's recaptured youth, no longer any need of idle speaking.

"She was the admirablest lady that ever lived: therefore, Master Doctor, if you will do us that favor, as to let us see that peerless dame, we should think ourselves much beholding unto you."

*T*here was a double wedding some two weeks later in the chapel at Longaville: and each marriage appears to have been happy enough.

The tenth Marquis of Falmouth had begotten sixteen children within seventeen years, at the end of which period his wife unluckily died in producing a final pledge of affection. This child, a daughter, survived, and was christened Cynthia: of her you may hear later.

Meanwhile the Earl and the Countess of Pevensey had propagated more moderately; and Pevensey had played a larger part in public life than was allotted to Falmouth, who did not shine at Court. Pevensey, indeed, has his sizable niche in history: his Irish expeditions, in 1575, were once notorious, as well as the circumstances of the earl's death in that year at Triloch Lenoch. His more famous son, then a boy of eight, succeeded to the title, and somewhat later, as the world knows, to the hazardous position of chief favorite to Queen Elizabeth.

"For Pevensey has the vision of a poet,"—thus Langard quotes the lonely old Queen,—"and to balance it, such mathematics as add two and two correctly, where you others smirk and assure me it sums up to whatever the Queen prefers. I have need of Pevensey: in this parched little age all England has need of Pevensey."

That is as it may have been: at all events, it is with this Lord Pevensey, at the height of his power, that we have now to do.

IX

The Episode Called Porcelain Cups

1. *Of Greatness Intimately Viewed*

"Ah, but they are beyond praise," said Cynthia Allonby, enraptured, "and certainly you should have presented them to the Queen."

"Her majesty already possesses a cup of that ware," replied Lord Pevensey. "It was one of her New Year's gifts, from Robert Cecil. Hers is, I believe, not quite so fine as either of yours; but then, they tell me, there is not the like of this pair in England, nor indeed on the hither side of Cataia."

He set the two pieces of Chinese pottery upon the shelves in the south corner of the room. These cups were of that sea-green tint called celadon, with a very wonderful glow and radiance. Such oddities were the last vogue at Court; and Cynthia could not but speculate as to what monstrous sum Lord Pevensey had paid for this his last gift to her.

Now he turned, smiling, a really superb creature in his blue and gold. "I had today another message from the Queen—"

"George," Cynthia said, with fond concern, "it frightens me to see you thus foolhardy, in tempting alike the Queen's anger and the Plague."

"Eh, as goes the Plague, it spares nine out of ten," he answered, lightly. "The Queen, I grant you, is another pair of sleeves, for an irritated Tudor spares nobody."

But Cynthia Allonby kept silence, and did not exactly smile, while she appraised her famous young kinsman. She was flattered by, and a little afraid of, the gay self-confidence which led anybody to take such chances. Two weeks ago it was that the terrible painted old Queen had named Lord Pevensey to go straightway into France, where, rumor had it, King Henri was preparing to renounce the Reformed Religion, and making his peace with the Pope: and for two weeks Pevensey had lingered, on one pretence or another, at his house in London, with the Plague creeping about the city like an invisible incalculable flame, and the Queen asking questions at Windsor. Of all the monarchs that had ever reigned in England, Elizabeth Tudor was the least used to having her orders disregarded. Meanwhile Lord Pevensey came every day to the Marquis of Falmouth's lodgings at Deptford: and every day Lord Pevensey pointed out to the marquis' daughter that Pevensey, whose wife had died in childbirth a year back, did not intend to go into France, for nobody could foretell how long a stay, as a widower. Certainly it was all very flattering. . .

"Yes, and you would be an excellent match," said Cynthia, aloud, "if that were all. And yet, what must I reasonably expect in marrying, sir, the famous Earl of Pevensey?"

"A great deal of love and petting, my dear. And if there were anything else to which you had a fancy, I would get it for you."

Her glance went to those lovely cups and lingered fondly. "Yes, dear Master Generosity, if it could be purchased or manufactured, you would get it for me—"

"If it exists I will get it for you," he declared.

"I think that it exists. But I am not learned enough to know what it is. George, if I married you I would have money and fine clothes and gilded coaches, and an army of maids and pages, and honor from all men. And you would be kind to me, I know, when you returned from the day's work at Windsor—or Holyrood or the Louvre. But do you not see that I would always be to you only a rather costly luxury, like those cups, which the Queen's minister could afford to keep for his hours of leisure?"

He answered: "You are all in all to me. You know it. Oh, very well do you know and abuse your power, you adorable and lovely baggage, who have kept me dancing attendance for a fortnight, without ever giving me an honest yes or no." He gesticulated. "Well, but life is very dull in Deptford village, and it amuses you to twist a Queen's adviser around your finger! I see it plainly, you minx, and I acquiesce because it delights me to give you pleasure, even at the cost of some dignity. Yet I may no longer shirk the Queen's business,—no, not even to amuse you, my dear."

"You said you had heard from her—again?"

"I had this morning my orders, under Gloriana's own fair hand, either to depart tomorrow into France or else to come tomorrow to Windsor. I need not say that in the circumstances I consider France the more wholesome."

Now the girl's voice was hurt and wistful. "So, for the thousandth time, is it proven the Queen's business means more to you than I do. Yes, certainly it is just as I said, George."

He observed, unruffled: "My dear, I scent unreason. This is a high matter. If the French King compounds with Rome, it means war for Protestant England. Even you must see that."

She replied, sadly: "Yes, even I! oh, certainly, my lord, even a half-witted child of seventeen can perceive as much as that."

"I was not speaking of half-witted persons, as I remember. Well, it chances that I am honored by the friendship of our gallant Bearnais, and am supposed to have some claim upon him, thanks to my good fortune last year in saving his life from the assassin Barriere. It chances that I may perhaps become, under providence, the instrument of preserving my fellow countrymen from much grief and trumpet-sounding and throat-cutting. Instead of pursuing that chance, two weeks ago—as was my duty—I have dangled at your apron-strings, in the vain hope of softening the most variable and hardest heart in the world. Now, clearly, I have not the right to do that any longer."

She admired the ennobled, the slightly rapt look which, she knew, denoted that George Bulmer was doing his duty as he saw it, even in her disappointment. "No, you have not the right. You are wedded to your statecraft, to your patriotism, to your self-advancement, or christen it what you will. You are wedded, at all events, to your man's business. You have not the time for such trifles as giving a maid that foolish and lovely sort of wooing to which every maid looks forward in her heart of hearts. Indeed, when you married the first time it was a kind of infidelity; and I am certain that poor, dear mouse-like Mary must have felt that often and over again. Why, do you not see, George, even now, that your wife will always come second to your real love?"

"In my heart, dear sophist, you will always come first. But it is not permitted that any loyal gentleman devote every hour of his life to sighing and making sonnets, and to the general solacing of a maid's loneliness in this dull little Deptford. Nor would you, I am sure, desire me to do so."

"I hardly know what I desire," she told him ruefully. "But I know that when you talk of your man's business I am lonely and chilled and far away from you. And I know that I cannot understand more than half your fine high notions about duty and patriotism and serving England and so on," the girl declared: and she flung wide her lovely little hands, in a despairing gesture. "I admire you, sir, when you talk of England. It makes you handsomer—yes, even handsomer!—somehow. But all the while I am remembering that England is just an ordinary island inhabited by a number of ordinary persons, for the most of whom I have no particular feeling one way or the other."

Pevensey looked down at her for a while with queer tenderness. Then he smiled. "No, I could not quite make you understand, my dear. But, ah, why fuddle that quaint little brain by trying to understand such matters as lie without your realm? For a woman's kingdom is the home, my dear, and her throne is in the heart of her husband—"

"All this is but another way of saying your lordship would have us cups upon a shelf," she pointed out—"in readiness for your leisure."

He shrugged, said "Nonsense!" and began more lightly to talk of other matters. Thus and thus he would do in France, such and such trinkets he would fetch back—"as toys for the most whimsical, the loveliest, and the most obstinate child in all the world," he phrased it. And they would be married, Pevensey declared, in September: nor (he gaily said) did he propose to have any further argument about it. Children should be seen— the proverb was dusty, but it particularly applied to pretty children.

Cynthia let him talk. She was just a little afraid of his self-confidence, and of this tall nobleman's habit of getting what he wanted, in the end: but she dispiritedly felt that Pevensey had failed her. Why, George Bulmer treated her as if she were a silly infant; and his want of her, even in that capacity, was a secondary matter: he was going into France, for all his petting talk, and was leaving her to shift as she best might, until he could spare the time to resume his love-making. . .

2. *What Comes of Scribbling*

Now when Pevensey had gone the room seemed darkened by the withdrawal of so much magnificence. Cynthia watched from the window as the tall earl rode away, with three handsomely clad retainers. Yes, George was very fine and admirable, no doubt of it: even so, there was relief in the reflection that for a month or two she was rid of him.

Turning, she faced a lean, dishevelled man, who stood by the Magdalen tapestry scratching his chin. He had unquiet bright eyes, this out-at-elbows poet whom a marquis' daughter was pleased to patronize, and his red hair was unpardonably tousled. Nor were his manners beyond reproach, for now, without saying anything, he, too, went to the window. He dragged one foot a little as he walked.

"So my lord Pevensey departs! Look how he rides in triumph! like lame Tamburlaine, with Techelles and Usumcasane and Theridamas to attend him, and with the sunset turning the dust raised by their horses' hoofs into a sort of golden haze about them. It is a beautiful world. And truly, Mistress Cyn," the poet said, reflectively, "that Pevensey is a very splendid ephemera. If not a king himself, at least he goes magnificently to settle the affairs of kings. Were modesty not my failing, Mistress Cyn, I would acclaim you as strangely lucky, in being beloved by two fine fellows that have not their like in England."

"Truly, you are not always thus modest, Kit Marlowe—"

"But, Lord, how seriously Pevensey takes it all! and takes himself in particular! Why, there departs from us, in befitting state, a personage whose opinion as to every topic in the world is written legibly in the carriage of those fine shoulders, even when seen from behind and from so considerable a distance. And in not one syllable do any of these opinions differ from the opinions of his great-great-grandfathers. Oho, and hark to Deptford! now all the oafs in the Corn-market are cheering this bulwark of Protestant England, this rising young hero of a people with no nonsense about them. Yes, it is a very quaint and rather splendid ephemera."

The daughter of a marquis could not quite approve of the way in which this shoemaker's son, however talented, railed at his betters. "Pevensey will be the greatest man in these kingdoms some day. Indeed, Kit Marlowe, there are those who say he is that much already."

"Oh, very probably! Still, I am puzzled by human greatness. A century hence what will he matter, this Pevensey? His ascent and his declension will have been completed, and his foolish battles and treaties will have given place to other foolish battles and treaties, and oblivion will have swallowed this glistening bluebottle, plumes and fine lace and stately ruff and all. Why, he is but an adviser to the queen of half an island, whereas my Tamburlaine was lord of all the golden ancient East: and what does my Tamburlaine matter now, save that he gave Kit Marlowe the subject of a drama? Hah, softly though! for does even that very greatly matter? Who really cares today about what scratches were made upon wax by that old Euripides, the latchet of whose sandals I am not worthy to unloose? No, not quite worthy, as yet!"

And thereupon the shabby fellow sat down in the tall leather-covered chair which Pevensey had just vacated: and this Marlowe nodded his flaming head portentously. "Hoh, look you, I am displeased, Mistress Cyn, I cannot lend my approval to this over-greedy oblivion that gapes for all. No, it is not a satisfying arrangement, that I should teeter insecurely through the void on a gob of mud, and be expected by and by to relinquish even that crazy foothold. Even for Kit Marlowe death lies in wait! and it may be, not anything more after death, not even any lovely words to play with. Yes, and this Marlowe may amount to nothing, after all: and his one chance of amounting to that which he intends may be taken away from him at any moment!"

He touched the breast of a weather-beaten doublet. He gave her that queer twisted sort of smile which the girl could not but find attractive, somehow. He said: "Why, but this heart thumping here inside me may stop any moment like a broken clock. Here is Euripides writing better than I: and here in my body, under my hand, is the mechanism upon which depend all those masterpieces that are to blot the Athenian from the reckoning, and I have no control of it!"

"Indeed, I fear that you control few things," she told him, "and that least of all do you control your taste for taverns and bad women. Oh, I hear tales of you!" And Cynthia raised a reproving forefinger.

"True tales, no doubt." He shrugged. "Lacking the moon he vainly cried for, the child learns to content himself with a penny whistle."

"Ah, but the moon is far away," the girl said, smiling—"too far to hear the sound of human crying: and besides, the moon, as I remember it, was never a very amorous goddess—"

"Just so," he answered: "also she was called Cynthia, and she, too, was beautiful."

"Yet is it the heart that cries to me, my poet?" she asked him, softly, "or just the lips?"

"Oh, both of them, most beautiful and inaccessible of goddesses." Then Marlowe leaned toward her, laughing and shaking that disreputable red head. "Still, you are very foolish, in your latest incarnation, to be wasting your rays upon carpet earls who will not outwear a century. Were modesty not my failing, I repeat, I could name somebody who will last longer. Yes, and—if but I lacked that plaguey virtue—I would advise you to go a-gypsying with that nameless somebody, so that two manikins might snatch their little share of the big things that are eternal, just as the butterfly fares intrepidly and joyously, with the sun for his torchboy, through a universe wherein thought cannot estimate the unimportance of a butterfly, and wherein not even the chaste moon is very important. Yes, certainly I would advise you to have done with this vanity of courts and masques, of satins and fans and fiddles, this dallying with tinsels and bright vapors;

and very movingly I would exhort you to seek out Arcadia, travelling hand in hand with that still nameless somebody." And of a sudden the restless man began to sing.

Sang Kit Marlowe:

> *"Come live with me and be my love,*
> *And we will all the pleasures prove*
> *That hills and valleys, dales and fields,*
> *Woods or steepy mountain yields.*
>
> *"And we will sit upon the rocks,*
> *And see the shepherds feed their flocks*
> *By shallow rivers, to whose falls*
> *Melodious birds sing madrigals—"*

But the girl shook her small, wise head decisively. "That is all very fine, but, as it happens, there is no such place as this Arcadia, where people can frolic in perpetual sunlight the year round, and find their food and clothing miraculously provided. No, nor can you, I am afraid, give me what all maids really, in their heart of hearts, desire far more than any sugar-candy Arcadia. Oh, as I have so often told you, Kit, I think you love no woman. You love words. And your seraglio is tenanted by very beautiful words, I grant you, though there is no longer any Sestos builded of agate and crystal, either, Kit Marlowe. For, as you may perceive, sir, I have read all that lovely poem you left with me last Thursday—"

She saw how interested he was, saw how he almost smirked. "Aha, so you think it not quite bad, eh, the conclusion of my *Hero and Leander*?"

"It is your best. And your middlemost, my poet, is better than aught else in English," she said, politely, and knowing how much he delighted to hear such remarks.

"Come, I retract my charge of foolishness, for you are plainly a wench of rare discrimination. And yet you say I do not love you! Cynthia, you are beautiful, you are perfect in all things. You are that heavenly Helen of whom I wrote, some persons say, acceptably enough. How strange it was I did not know that Helen was dark-haired and pale! for certainly yours is that immortal loveliness which must be served by poets in life and death."

"And I wonder how much of these ardors," she thought, "is kindled by my praise of his verses?" She bit her lip, and she regarded him with a hint of sadness. She said, aloud: "But I did not, after all, speak to Lord Pevensey concerning the printing of your poem. Instead, I burned your *Hero and Leander*."

She saw him jump, as under a whip-lash. Then he smiled again, in that wry fashion of his. "I lament the loss to letters, for it was my only copy. But you knew that."

"Yes, Kit, I knew it was your only copy."

"Oho! and for what reason did you burn it, may one ask?"

"I thought you loved it more than you loved me. It was my rival, I thought—" The girl was conscious of remorse, and yet it was remorse commingled with a mounting joy.

"And so you thought a jingle scribbled upon a bit of paper could be your rival with me!"

Then Cynthia no longer doubted, but gave a joyous little sobbing laugh, for the love of her disreputable dear poet was sustaining the stringent testing she had devised. She touched his freckled hand caressingly, and her face was as no man had ever seen it, and her voice, too, caressed him.

"Ah, you have made me the happiest of women, Kit! Kit, I am almost disappointed in you, though, that you do not grieve more for the loss of that beautiful poem."

His smiling did not waver; yet the lean, red-haired man stayed motionless. "Why, but see how lightly I take the destruction of my life-work in this, my masterpiece! For I can assure you it was a masterpiece, the fruit of two years' toil and of much loving repolishment—"

"Ah, but you love me better than such matters, do you not?" she asked him, tenderly. "Kit Marlowe, I adore you! Sweetheart, do you not understand that a woman wants to be loved utterly and entirely? She wants no rivals, not even paper rivals. And so often when you talked of poetry I have felt lonely and chilled and far away from you, and I have been half envious, dear, of your Heros and Helens and your other good-for-nothing Greek minxes. But now I do not mind them at all. And I will make amends, quite prodigal amends, for my naughty jealousy: and my poet shall write me some more lovely poems, so he shall—"

He said: "You fool!"

And she drew away from him, for this man was no longer smiling.

"You burned my *Hero and Leander*! You! you big-eyed fool! You lisping idiot! you wriggling, cuddling worm! you silken bag of guts! had not even you the wit to perceive it was immortal beauty which would have lived long after you and I were stinking dirt? And you, a half-witted animal, a shining, chattering parrot, lay claws to it!" Marlowe had risen in a sort of seizure, in a condition which was really quite unreasonable when you considered that only a poem was at stake, even a rather long poem.

And Cynthia began to smile, with tremulous hurt-looking young lips. "So my poet's love is very much the same as Pevensey's love! And I was right, after all."

"Oh, oh!" said Marlowe, "that ever a poet should love a woman! What jokes does the lewd flesh contrive!" Of a sudden he was calmer; and then rage fell away from him like a dropped cloak, and he viewed her as with respectful wonder. "Why, but you sitting there, with goggling innocent bright eyes, are an allegory of all that is most droll and tragic. Yes, and indeed there is no reason to blame you. It is not your fault that every now and then is born a man who serves an idea which is to him the most important thing in the world. It is not your fault that this man perforce inhabits a body to which the most important thing in the world is a woman. Certainly it is not your fault that this compost makes yet another jumble of his two desires, and persuades himself that the two are somehow allied. The woman inspires, the woman uplifts, the woman strengthens him for his high work, saith he! Well, well, perhaps there are such women, but by land and sea I have encountered none of them."

All this was said while Marlowe shuffled about the room, with bent shoulders, and nodding his tousled red head, and limping as he walked. Now Marlowe turned, futile and shabby looking, just where a while ago Lord Pevensey had loomed resplendent. Again she saw the poet's queer, twisted, jeering smile.

"What do you care for my ideals? What do you care for the ideals of that tall earl whom for a fortnight you have held from his proper business? or for the ideals of any man alive? Why, not one thread of that dark hair, not one snap of those white little fingers, except when ideals irritate you by distracting a man's attention from Cynthia Allonby. Otherwise, he is welcome enough to play with his incomprehensible toys."

He jerked a thumb toward the shelves behind him.

"Oho, you virtuous pretty ladies! what all you value is such matters as those cups: they please the eye, they are worth sound money, and people envy you the possession of them. So you cherish your shiny mud cups, and you burn my *Hero and Leander*: and I declaim all this dull nonsense over the ashes of my ruined dreams, thinking at bottom of how pretty you are, and of how much I would like to kiss you. That is the real tragedy, the immemorial tragedy, that I should still hanker after you, my Cynthia—"

His voice dwelt tenderly upon her name. His fever-haunted eyes were tender, too, for just a moment. Then he grimaced.

"No, I was wrong—the tragedy strikes deeper. The root of it is that there is in you and in all your glittering kind no malice, no will to do harm nor to hurt anything, but just a bland and invincible and, upon the whole, a well-meaning stupidity, informing a bright and soft and delicately scented animal. So you work ruin among those men who serve ideals, not foreplanning ruin, not desiring to ruin anything, not even having sufficient wit to perceive the ruin when it is accomplished. You are, when all is done, not even detestable, not even a worthy peg whereon to hang denunciatory sonnets, you shallow-pated pretty creatures whom poets—oh, and in youth all men are poets!—whom poets, now and always, are doomed to hanker after to the detriment of their poesy. No, I concede it: you kill without pre-meditation, and without ever suspecting your hands to be anything but stainless. So in logic I must retract all my harsh words; and I must, without any hint of reproach, endeavor to bid you a somewhat more civil farewell."

She had regarded him, throughout this preposterous and uncalled-for harangue, with sad composure, with a forgiving pity. Now she asked him, very quietly, "Where are you going, Kit?"

"To the Golden Hind, O gentle, patient and unjustly persecuted virgin martyr!" he answered, with an exaggerated bow—"since that is the part in which you now elect to posture."

"Not to that low, vile place again!"

"But certainly I intend in that tavern to get tipsy as quickly as possible: for then the first woman I see will for the time become the woman whom I desire, and who exists nowhere." And with that the red-haired man departed, limping and singing as he went to look for a trull in a pot-house.

Sang Kit Marlowe:

> "And I will make her beds of roses
> And a thousand fragrant posies;
> A cap of flowers, and a kirtle
> Embroidered all with leaves of myrtle.

"A gown made of the finest wool
Which from our pretty lambs we pull;
Fair-lined slippers for the cold,
With buckles of the purest gold—"

3. *Economics of Egeria*

SHE SAT QUITE STILL WHEN Marlowe had gone.

"He will get drunk again," she thought despondently. "Well, and why should it matter to me if he does, after all that outrageous ranting? He has been unforgivably insulting—Oh, but none the less, I do not want to have him babbling of the roses and gold of that impossible fairy world which the poor, frantic child really believes in, to some painted woman of the town who will laugh at him. I loathe the thought of her laughing at him—and kissing him! His notions are wild foolishness; but I at least wish that they were not foolishness, and that hateful woman will not care one way or the other."

So Cynthia sighed, and to comfort her forlorn condition fetched a hand-mirror from the shelves whereon glowed her green cups. She touched each cup caressingly in passing; and that which she found in the mirror, too, she regarded not unappreciatively, from varying angles. . . Yes, after all, dark hair and a pale skin had their advantages at a court where pink and yellow women were so much the fashion as to be common. Men remembered you more distinctively.

Though nobody cared for men, in view of their unreasonable behavior, and their absolute self-centeredness. . . Oh, it was pitiable, it was grotesque, she reflected sadly, how Pevensey and Kit Marlowe had both failed her, after so many pretty speeches.

Still, there was a queer pleasure in being wooed by Kit: his insane notions went to one's head like wine. She would send Meg for him again tomorrow. And Pevensey was, of course, the best match imaginable. . . No, it would be too heartless to dismiss George Buhner outright. It was unreasonable of him to desert her because a Gascon threatened to go to mass: but, after all, she would probably marry George, in the end. He was really almost unendurably silly, though, about England and freedom and religion and right and wrong and things like that. Yes, it would be tedious to have a husband who often talked to you as though he were addressing a public assemblage. . . Yet, he was very handsome, particularly in his highflown and most tedious moments; that year-old son of his was sickly, and would probably die soon, the sweet forlorn little pet, and not be a bother to anybody: and her dear old father would be profoundly delighted by the marriage of his daughter to a man whose wife could have at will a dozen céladon cups, and anything else she chose to ask for. . .

But now the sun had set, and the room was growing quite dark. So Cynthia stood a-tiptoe, and replaced the mirror upon the shelves, setting it upright behind those wonderful green cups which had anew reminded her of Pevensey's wealth and generosity. She smiled a little, to think of what fun it had been to hold George back, for two whole weeks, from discharging that horrible old queen's stupid errands.

4. *Treats Philosophically of Breakage*

THE DOOR OPENED. STALWART YOUNG Captain Edward Musgrave came with a lighted candle, which he placed carefully upon the table in the room's centre.

He said: "They told me you were here. I come from London. I bring news for you."

"You bring no pleasant tidings, I fear—"

"As Lord Pevensey rode through the Strand this afternoon, on his way home, the Plague smote him. That is my sad news. I grieve to bring such news, for your cousin was a worthy gentleman and universally respected."

"Ah," Cynthia said, very quiet, "so Pevensey is dead. But the Plague kills quickly!"

"Yes, yes, that is a comfort, certainly. Yes, he turned quite black in the face, they report, and before his men could reach him had fallen from his horse. It was all over almost instantly. I saw him afterward, hardly a pleasant sight. I came to you as soon as I could. I was vexatiously detained—"

"So George Bulmer is dead, in a London gutter! It seems strange, because he was here, befriended by monarchs, and very strong and handsome and self-confident, hardly two hours ago. Is that his blood upon your sleeve?"

"But of course not! I told you I was vexatiously detained, almost at your gates. Yes, I had the ill luck to blunder into a disgusting business. The two rapscallions tumbled out of a doorway under my horse's very nose, egad! It was a near thing I did not ride them down. So I stopped, naturally. I regretted stopping, afterward, for I was too late to be of help. It was at the Golden Hind, of course. Something really ought to be done about that place. Yes, and that rogue Marler bled all over a new doublet, as you see. And the Deptford constables held me with their foolish interrogatories—"

"So one of the fighting men was named Marlowe! Is he dead, too, dead in another gutter?"

"Marlowe or Marler, or something of the sort—wrote plays and sonnets and such stuff, they tell me. I do not know anything about him—though, I give you my word, now, those greasy constables treated me as though I were a noted frequenter of pot-houses. That sort of thing is most annoying. At all events, he was drunk as David's sow, and squabbling over, saving your presence, a woman of the sort one looks to find in that abominable hole. And so, as I was saying, this other drunken rascal dug a knife into him—"

But now, to Captain Musgrave's discomfort, Cynthia Allonby had begun to weep heartbrokenly.

So he cleared his throat, and he patted the back of her hand. "It is a great shock to you, naturally—oh, most naturally, and does you great credit. But come now, Pevensey is gone, as we must all go some day, and our tears cannot bring him back, my dear. We can but hope he is better off, poor fellow, and look on it as a mysterious dispensation and that sort of thing, my dear—"

"Oh, Ned, but people are so cruel! People will be saying that it was I who kept poor Cousin George in London this past two weeks, and that but for me he would have been in France long ago! And then the Queen, Ned!—why, that pig-headed old woman will be blaming it on me, that there is nobody to prevent that detestable French King from turning Catholic and dragging England into new wars, and I shall not be able to go to any of the Court dances! nor to the masques!" sobbed Cynthia, "nor anywhere!"

"Now you talk tender-hearted and angelic nonsense. It is noble of you to feel that way, of course. But Pevensey did not take proper care of himself, and that is all there is to it. Now I have remained in London since the Plague's outbreak. I stayed with my regiment, naturally. We have had a few deaths, of course. People die everywhere. But the Plague has never bothered me. And why has it never bothered me? Simply because I was sensible, took the pains to consult an astrologer, and by his advice wear about my neck, night and day, a bag containing tablets of toads' blood and arsenic. It is an infallible specific for men born in February. No, not for a moment do I wish to speak harshly of the dead, but sensible persons cannot but consider Lord Pevensey's death to have been caused by his own carelessness."

"Now, certainly that is true," the girl said, brightening. "It was really his own carelessness and his dear lovable rashness. And somebody could explain it to the Queen. Besides, I often think that wars are good for the public spirit of a nation, and bring out its true manhood. But then it upset me, too, a little, Ned, to hear about this Marlowe—for I must tell you that I knew the poor man, very slightly. So I happen to know that today he flung off in a rage, and began drinking, because somebody, almost by pure chance, had burned a packet of his verses—"

Thereupon Captain Musgrave raised heavy eyebrows, and guffawed so heartily that the candle flickered. "To think of the fellow's putting it on that plea! when he could so easily have written some more verses. That is the trouble with these poets, if you ask me: they are not practical even in their ordinary everyday lying. No, no, the truth of it was that the rogue wanted a pretext for making a beast of himself, and seized the first that came to hand. Egad, my dear, it is a daily practise with these poets. They hardly draw a sober breath. Everybody knows that."

Cynthia was looking at him in the half-lit room with very flattering admiration. . . Seen thus, with her scarlet lips a little parted—disclosing pearls,—and with her naive dark eyes aglow, she was quite incredibly pretty and caressable. She had almost forgotten until now that this stalwart soldier, too, was in love with her. But now her spirits were rising venturously, and she knew that she liked Ned Musgrave. He had sensible notions; he saw things as they really were, and with him there would never be any nonsense about toplofty ideas. Then, too, her dear old white-haired father would be pleased, because there was a very fair estate. . .

So Cynthia said: "I believe you are right, Ned. I often wonder how they can be so lacking in self-respect. Oh, I am certain you must be right, for it is just what I felt without being able quite to express it. You will stay for supper with us, of course. Yes, but you must, because it is always a great comfort for me to talk with really sensible persons. I do not wonder that you are not very eager to stay, though, for I am probably a fright, with my eyes red, and with my hair all tumbling down, like an old witch's. Well, let us see what can be done about it, sir! There was a hand-mirror—"

And thus speaking, she tripped, with very much the reputed grace of a fairy, toward the far end of the room, and standing a-tiptoe, groped at the obscure shelves, with a resultant crash of falling china.

"Oh, but my lovely cups!" said Cynthia, in dismay. "I had forgotten they were up there: and now I have smashed both of them, in looking for my mirror, sir, and trying to prettify myself for you. And I had so fancied them, because they had not their like in England!"

She looked at the fragments, and then at Musgrave, with wide, innocent hurt eyes. She was really grieved by the loss of her quaint toys. But Musgrave, in his sturdy, common-sense way, only laughed at her seriousness over such kickshaws.

"I am for an honest earthenware tankard myself!" he said, jovially, as the two went in to supper.

1905–1919

"Tell me where is fancy bred Or in the heart or in the head? How begot, how nourished? . . . Then let us all ring fancy's knell."

X

The Envoi Called Semper Idem

1. *Which Baulks at an Estranging Sea*

Here, then, let us end the lovers' comedy, after a good precedent, with supper as the denouement. *Chacun ira souper: la comédie ne peut pas mieux finir.*

For epilogue, Cynthia Allonby was duly married to Edward Musgrave, and he made her a fair husband, as husbands go. That was the upshot of Pevensey's death and Marlowe's murder: as indeed, it was the outcome of all the earlier-recorded heart-burnings and endeavors and spoiled dreams. Through generation by generation, traversing just three centuries, I have explained to you, my dear Mrs. Grundy, how divers weddings came about: and each marriage appears, upon the whole, to have resulted satisfactorily. Dame Melicent and Dame Adelaide, not Florian, touched the root of the matter as they talked together at Storisende: and the trio's descendants could probe no deeper.

But now we reach the annals of the house of Musgrave: and further adventuring is blocked by R. V. Musgrave's monumental work *The Musgraves of Matocton*. The critical may differ as to the plausibility of the family tradition (ably defended by Colonel Musgrave, pp. 33–41) that Mistress Cynthia Musgrave was the dark lady of Shakespeare's Sonnets, and that this poet, also, in the end, absolved her of intentional malice. There is none, at any event, but may find in this genealogical classic a full record of the highly improbable happenings which led to the emigration of Captain Edward Musgrave, and later of Cynthia Musgrave, to the Colony of Virginia; and none but must admire Colonel Musgrave's painstaking and accurate tracing of the American Musgraves who descended from this couple, down to the eve of the twentieth century.

It would be supererogatory, therefore, for me to tell you of the various Musgrave marriages, and to re-dish such data as is readily accessible on the reference shelves of the nearest public library, as well as in the archives of the Colonial Dames, of the Society of the Cincinnati, and of the Sons and Daughters of various wars. It suffices that from the marriage of Edward Musgrave and Cynthia Allonby sprang this well-known American family, prolific of brave gentlemen and gracious ladies who in due course, and in new lands, achieved their allotted portion of laughter and anguish and compromise, very much as their European fathers and mothers had done aforetime.

So I desist to follow the line of love across the Atlantic; and, for the while at least, make an end of these chronicles. My pen flags, my ink runs low, and (since Florian wedded twice) the Dizain of Marriages is completed.

2. *Which Defers to Various Illusions*

I HAVE BOUND UP MY gleanings from the fields of old years into a modest sheaf; and if it be so fortunate as to please you, my dear Mrs. Grundy,—if it so come about that your ladyship be moved in time to desire another sheaf such as this,—why, assuredly, my surprise will be untempered with obduracy. The legends of Allonby have been but lightly touched upon: and apart from the *Aventures d'Adhelmar*, Nicolas de Caen is thus far represented in English only by the *Roi Atnaury* (which, to be sure, is Nicolas' masterpiece) and the mutilated *Dizain des Reines* and the fragmentary *Roman de Lusignan*.

But since you, madam, are not Schahriah, to give respite for the sake of an unnarrated tale, I must now without further peroration make an end. Through the monstrous tapestry I have traced out for you the windings of a single thread, and I entreat you, dear lady, to accept it with assurances of my most distinguished regard.

And if the offering be no great gift, this lack of greatness, believe me, is due to the errors and limitations of the transcriber alone.

For they loved greatly, these men and women of the past, in that rapt hour wherein Nature tricked them to noble ends, and lured them to skyey heights of adoration and sacrifice. At bottom they were, perhaps, no more heroical than you or I. Indeed, neither Florian nor Adhelmar was at strict pains to act as common-sense dictated, and Falstaff is scarcely describable as immaculate: Villon thieved, Kit Marlowe left a wake of emptied bottles, and Will Sommers was notoriously a fool; Matthiette was vain, and Adelais self-seeking, and the tenth Marquis of Falmouth, if you press me, rather a stupid and pompous ass: and yet to each in turn it was granted to love greatly, to know at least one hour of magnanimity when each was young in the world's annually recaptured youth.

And if that hour did not ever have its sequel in precisely the anticipated life-long rapture, nor always in a wedding with the person preferred, yet since at any rate it resulted in a marriage that turned out well enough, in a world wherein people have to consider expediency, one may rationally assert that each of these romances ended happily. Besides, there had been the hour.

Ah, yes, this love is an illusion, if you will. Wise men have protested that vehemently enough in all conscience. But there are two ends to every stickler for his opinion here. Whether you see, in this fleet hour's abandonment to love, the man's spark of divinity flaring in momentary splendor,—a tragic candle, with divinity guttering and half-choked among the drossier particles, and with momentary splendor lighting man's similitude to Him in Whose likeness man was created,—or whether you, more modernly, detect as prompting this surrender coarse-fibred Nature, in the Prince of Lycia's role (with all mankind her Troiluses to be cajoled into perpetuation of mankind), you have, in either event, conceded that to live unbefooled by love is at best a shuffling and debt-dodging business, and you have granted this unreasoned, transitory surrender to be the most high and, indeed, the one requisite action which living affords.

Beyond that is silence. If you succeed in proving love a species of madness, you have but demonstrated that there is something more profoundly pivotal than sanity, and for the sanest logician this is a disastrous gambit: whereas if, in well-nigh obsolete fashion, you confess the universe to be a weightier matter than the contents of your skull, and your wits a somewhat slender instrument wherewith to plumb infinity,—why, then you will recall that it is written *God is love*, and this recollection, too, is conducive to a fine taciturnity.

A Note About the Author

James Branch Cabell (1879–1958) was an American writer of escapist and fantasy fiction. Born into a wealthy family in the state of Virginia, Cabell attended the College of William and Mary, where he graduated in 1898 following a brief personal scandal. His first stories began to be published, launching a productive decade in which Cabell's worked appeared in both *Harper's Monthly Magazine* and *The Saturday Evening Post*. Over the next forty years, Cabell would go on to publish fifty-two books, many of them novels and short-story collections. A friend, colleague, and inspiration to such writers as Ellen Glasgow, H.L. Mencken, Sinclair Lewis, and Theodore Dreiser, James Branch Cabell is remembered as an iconoclastic pioneer of fantasy literature.

A Note from the Publisher

Spanning many genres, from non-fiction essays to literature classics to children's books and lyric poetry, Mint Edition books showcase the master works of our time in a modern new package. The text is freshly typeset, is clean and easy to read, and features a new note about the author in each volume. Many books also include exclusive new introductory material. Every book boasts a striking new cover, which makes it as appropriate for collecting as it is for gift giving. Mint Edition books are only printed when a reader orders them, so natural resources are not wasted. We're proud that our books are never manufactured in excess and exist only in the exact quantity they need to be read and enjoyed.

bookfinity™

Discover more of your favorite classics with Bookfinity™.

- Track your reading with custom book lists.
- Get great book recommendations for your personalized Reader Type.
- Add reviews for your favorite books.
- AND MUCH MORE!

Visit **bookfinity.com** and take the fun Reader Type quiz to get started.

Enjoy our classic and modern companion pairings!

Classic & Modern

Printed in the USA
CPSIA information can be obtained
at www.ICGtesting.com
JSHW022340140824
68134JS00019B/1605